The Beast of Baloddan

Andy Cutbill

*Hodder
Children's
Books*

A division of Hodder Headline Limited

For Charlie, proofreader extraordinaire

First published in Great Britain in 2003
by Hodder Children's Books

A Catalogue record for this book is available
from the British Library

ISBN 0 340 86570 9

Typeset by Avon Dataset Ltd, Bidford-on-Avon, Warks

Printed and bound in Great Britain by
Clays Ltd, St Ives plc

The paper and board used in this paperback by Hodder
Children's Books are natural recyclable products made from
wood grown in sustainable forests. The manufacturing
processes conform to the environmental regulations
of the country of origin.

Hodder Children's Books
a division of Hodder Headline Limited
338 Euston Road
London NW1 3BH

For more information on Andy Cutbill, visit:
www.rippinggags.co.uk

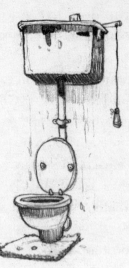

Chapter One

'Miaow. Miaow. Miaow. Miaow . . .'

Mr Whicker was a peculiar gentleman. At seventy-three, he was slightly bent over and would shuffle around his dusty grocery shop in his slippers, miaowing like a cat. He didn't *have* any cats, in fact he collected porcelain hedgehogs, but miaowing was better than barking. Mr Whicker detested dogs.

When the bell above the door tinkled on that sunny July morning, Mr Whicker was busy at his printing press in the small room at the back of his shop. As the ancient machine sucked and whistled, sweeping in sheets of paper one end and regurgitating them out the other, the grocer leant around the narrow door to see who'd entered. The shop however seemed to be empty. The bell jingled again as the door closed.

'Mothballs,' came a quiet voice.

The voice sounded familiar. Cheerful, but softly spoken. Whicker shuffled out to the counter, but still he couldn't see anybody.

'Hmm, toilet bleach, fly spray . . . ah. Mothballs.'

'Can I help you?' asked Whicker, rather baffled.

'No, I'm fine thanks,' called the voice from behind a far shelf.

The grocer sidestepped the floor mop display and made his way out to the front of the shop. He noticed an old bicycle leaning up against the outside wall.

'Have you got any lard?' came the voice.

Whicker peered through the mango chutney jars on the 'durable goods' shelf. He jumped as he found a pair of eyes glaring out at him.

'I think we've run out,' he said.

'Right.'

The customer crossed 'lard' off his shopping list. As the eyes disappeared Mr Whicker caught a flash of black hair. It was scruffy, and whoever it belonged to was shorter than he was expecting. Mr Whicker followed the sound of the customer's breathing, his head bobbing as he tried to catch a glimpse of the mystery person through the cereal boxes.

'Nylon stockings, three pairs.'

'Bottom shelf,' called out Whicker, and he

immediately knelt down and peered through the bin liners. He could just make out the soles of a pair of well-worn trainers.

'Right. One, two, three pairs.'

The customer stood up and marched off down the aisle. The shopkeeper tried to keep up on his hands and knees. They met each other at the end of the row.

'Argh!' yelped Whicker, falling back on to his bottom. The customer was a boy of about ten. He was wearing a pair of jeans, faded at the knees, and an old T-shirt. He had a bicycle helmet under one arm and a shopping basket in the other hand.

'Ah, good golly,' panted Whicker, clutching his chest. 'Robert Twistleton. I thought you were . . . erm. Someone else.'

'Sorry, Mr Whicker.' The boy grinned and placed the basket on to the counter in front of him.

The shopkeeper slowly got up, and worked his way round to the till, still panting. 'Shouldn't you be at school, young man?' he asked.

'First day of the holidays,' said Bert cheerfully. 'Mum's getting ready for all the guests to arrive; summer season starts today.'

'Ah. Of course. Better stock up on wet weather gear,' mumbled Whicker. 'Bound to rain once Baloddan's full of tourists.'

Bert dug deep into his pockets and pulled out a few coins, which clattered as he placed them on the desk.

'Is all this for your mum then?' asked Whicker, daintily examining a pot of leg wax.

'My grandfather actually.'

Whicker peered at the boy over the top of his spectacles. 'Your grandfather?' he asked, frowning.

'Yup.'

'Right. Of course,' he said, and he dropped the pot into the bag.

With a final cough the till spat out the cash tray and Mr Whicker rifled around for some change. Bert shoved it into his pocket, grabbed the bag and made for the door.

'Send my regards to your family,' called Whicker as the doorbell jingled once again. 'And your grandfather.'

'Will do,' called Robert. 'Say hello to the cats.'

'Cats?' mumbled Whicker. 'What cats?'

Outside in the sunshine, Bert took a breath of the Cornish sea air. Nothing beat the feeling of the beginning of the school holidays. Two months of freedom, even though home would be full of a few hundred paying guests.

He climbed on to his bicycle, hooked the bag through the handlebars and pushed himself off down the lane. As he rattled his way through the cobbled village, along the harbour wall where the rigging of the fishing boats chattered in the breeze, the houses began to thin out. Soon he was out into the open countryside, with the sunshine hot on his back. There were few trees out here, just the tussock grass and one or two gorse bushes. Over to his right Bert could see the cliff path and the sea, and way in the distance, out on the point, he could just make out the Baloddan Hotel, jutting out into the blue sky. Home, he thought.

'Get out the road, imbecile!'

Bert almost fell off his bike. Twisting around, he found an enormous coach speeding towards him. As he swerved, his front tyre caught in a pothole and he landed head first in the tussock grass by the side of the road. The coach thundered past, its wheels missing the bike by inches. Looking up, Bert could just make out a dozen faces pressed up against the back window. *WAAAH WAAH* went the horn, jeering at him. He climbed to his feet and brushed himself down.

Idiots, he thought.

The foyer on the ground floor of the hotel was vast. It more closely resembled the booking hall of a grand train station than a place where hotel guests came to check in. Bert had leant the bike against the wall by the hotel porch, and now, having swung through the double front doors, he scanned the crowd for anyone he recognized. A long queue wound its way back from the desk, over the colourful mosaic scene of Baloddan harbour tiled on the huge floor. The Coldstream Guards Band, playing 'One Hundred and One Marching Classics', was blaring out of the tannoy system. Bert's dad was mad keen on military music. It drove his mum spare.

As he fought his way through the holidaymakers, his trainers squeaking on the tiles, he had the uneasy feeling of hundreds of pairs of eyes staring at him.

'Isn't that the boy that was cycling down the middle of the road, Sydney?' someone croaked.

'Scruffy little oik,' came the reply.

In the far corner of the room, a door with the words PRIVATE, NO ADMITTANCE written in stern red letters signified the entrance into the Twistleton apartment. Bert pushed his way through. *Thwatthwat* went the door as it bounced back on its sprung hinges.

On the other side things were quieter. Cooler even. The apartment hall was large and square with a stone floor. Various rooms came off it, with a dark stairwell built into the far wall, which dropped down into the hotel basements, and a giant grandfather clock that ticked noisily in the corner. Behind him, Bert could still hear the marching music, but closer by was the muffled din of his father singing along.

Bert opened the door into the sitting room. 'Grandpa?' he called. Empty. Bert went through into the kitchen. 'Grandpa, I've got your things.'

Suddenly there was a dull thud from below.

'BLAST IT!' he heard his father swear. 'Wretched pipes.'

Bert imagined his dad rubbing his bald head. The hotel plumbing was well known for being a hazard. The archaic maze of Victorian lead pipes bucked and dived and wound their way around the entire building before they eventually dropped down into the basements.

'Grandpa? Gaffer? I've got your shopping.'

'Robert? Is that you?' came a voice from the bathroom. It was Edith, Bert's grandmother. 'Your grandfather's downstairs. Something about fixing one of the boilers in the lower basement. You can give the shopping to me though, I'll be out in a minute.'

Bert sighed and sat on the stone floor opposite the bathroom door and waited for his grandmother to come out. As he closed his eyes and relaxed, he could hear her soft, familiar humming which had so often sung him to sleep in the past.

CRASH! Bert woke up with a start. He didn't know how long he'd been dozing. The marching music was still playing, but his grandmother's humming had stopped.

'Granny?' he said. Waiting a moment, he tested the door. It was still locked. Bert tapped lightly on the frosted glass window. 'Are you all right in there?'

Silence. And then a low, gut-wrenching groan of stretching, yawning metal that shook the lead pipes circling the hallway. The door handle shuddered.

Bert frowned. 'Granny?' he said, now a little more concerned. 'Are you all right?'

'Robert?' came his grandmother's voice. 'I think I might need some help.'

BOOM! An eruption of water like a geyser exploding out of the ground shook the bathroom door. Slime oozed out into the hallway. Bert shook the door handle as he heard his granny gurgling inside.

'Help!' cried Bert. 'Somebody help.'

But the Coldstream Guards were playing louder, as if someone was purposefully turning the music up, masking Bert's cries. As the moaning grew, the pane of glass darkened and water and slime spewed out on to the corridor tiles around Bert's feet. Bert took a step back and charged at the bathroom door. It wouldn't budge. Again he threw his weight at it and this time the door burst open. As Bert slid across the floor, the roaring stopped and was replaced by a terrific suction and rush of wind (like flushing the loo on an aeroplane). As he landed in a heap under the sink, he frantically looked around him. The whole room was dripping with muck. The walls were thick with purple mucus, and a black sludge seeped out from the toilet cistern. And all that was left of Edith Twistleton was her pair of shoes, sitting exactly where they had been when her feet were still in them.

Bert wiped some sludge from his face. It had got in his ears, in his hair and even in his mouth. It tasted vile. He got to his feet and carefully slid over to the toilet. There was a faint sucking, growing more and more distant, and Bert could feel a draught on the back of his neck as air was dragged down into the toilet bowl and around the U-bend.

And then Bert heard the last of his granny: a single word that sounded as if it had come from hundreds of miles away; a whisper that could have been mistaken for the howling wind.

'Robert,' cried the voice.

And then silence.

Chapter Two

The kink in the cliff path, where the headland reached its most westerly point, had long been a refuge for Bert when he needed time to think. The views were spectacular from here. If he screwed up his eyes he could see from the village of Baloddan to the north, to the old chapel on the cliff edge half a mile away to the south. And in fine weather it was sometimes possible to spot oil tankers out on the horizon as they crawled their way towards the Bristol Channel.

The week since his grandmother's disappearance had been difficult and confusing, and as he lay across the path – with his feet in the tussock grass and his head perched on his hands, looking out over the cliff edge – Bert tried desperately to find some sort of explanation of its grim events.

'A massive back draught from an internal explosion caused by the build up of methane gases in the hotel sewers,' said the police officer, sticking out his chest.

Bert looked at him blankly.

'Your grandmother was sucked down the toilet, Robert. Bottom first.'

The policeman, a tall gentleman with thick black hairs protruding from both nostrils, seemed almost to be enjoying himself as he spat out the gory details. Robert shifted uneasily. His bottom had gone numb from sitting on the hard kitchen chair for too long, so he'd sat on his hands in an effort to regain some feeling. Now all the blood seemed to be draining from his fingers.

'Please concentrate, Robert,' pleaded Bert's mother weakly, sitting at the other side of the table. She looked pale, and her make-up had run where she'd been crying. The news of her mother-in-law's death had hit her hard.

'We need to understand exactly what happened,' she said, her voice almost a whisper. 'It's important, Robert.'

The clock on the wall read twenty past three. Bert had been found by his grandfather, who'd managed to pick him up off the floor and drag him out into

11

the hallway. Apparently he'd fainted beside the loo.

The policeman leant across the table and eyeballed Bert.

'Robert, you say there was slime all over the walls and the floor.' He consulted his notes. ' "Black goo, loads of it, coming from under the cistern lid." '

Bert nodded. 'I slipped,' he said, and felt the lump on his head where he'd hit the sink. He grimaced with pain.

The policeman glanced at Bert's mother, who got out of her chair and made her way around the table. 'Robert,' she said, kneeling by his side, 'the bathroom was completely clean when we found you. There wasn't any evidence of the *slime* at all. Just your grandmother's shoes.' She took Bert's hand. 'Are you sure you're telling the truth?'

'If you're making this all up, son,' said the policeman gravely, 'you'll be in serious trouble.'

Bert thought for a while. His mother went to the window and looked out over the cliffs.

'Where's Dad?' Bert asked softly.

'He's gone to comfort your grandfather,' said his mum.

The policeman closed his notebook and placed a hand on Mrs Twistleton's shoulder. They both walked out into the hallway.

'Well, at least your son seems all right,' Bert heard the officer say. 'I don't think he's trying to be difficult. Just a nasty case of shock, that's all.

Post-traumatic stress syndrome is only to be expected after such an appalling experience. Of course, he should see a doctor for a proper diagnosis.'

The seagulls were gathering above the cliffs now, fat with the scraps that they'd scavenged from the fishing trawlers making their way into port. As the gulls wheeled and hung on the breeze, squawking and screeching before they dived down to their nests below the cliff edge, Bert turned on to his back and rested his arms behind his head. And just as the warm sun fell upon his face, the local priest crashed into him on his bicycle.

'Whooooooooaa!' screamed the priest, as he was thrown straight over the handlebars and into a clump of stinging nettles.

Bert, meanwhile, was entangled in the working parts of the bicycle; his hair had caught in the chain and his right trouser leg in the spokes of the back wheel. As hard as he fought, he couldn't get out from underneath. It was with one last terrific kick that he eventually freed himself and sent the priest's shiny bicycle sailing straight over the cliff edge. He watched in horror as the bike somersaulted down the rock face and landed in a heap on the beach below.

Bert rubbed his head.

'Ahhh, I'm being stung! Help me!' hollered the priest from the nettle patch.

Father Hooper was a tall man with a hooked nose and a shock of thick black hair that looked like he'd stuck his fingers in a plug socket. Dressed in a black tunic and cape, he had been carrying a pile of thick brown ledgers in the woven basket on the front of his bike. They now littered the gorse bushes beside the path. Bert brushed himself down and went to give the priest a hand.

'Get off, you imbecile!' screamed Father Hooper, waving his arms around as though he was trying to fend off an army. 'Can't you see you've done enough damage for one morning?'

Bert let go of the priest, who immediately fell back into the nettles, and started to pick up a few of the books. They were old and dusty with thick leather covers. He began to open one up.

'Leave those alone, you little busybody,' snapped Hooper, climbing to his feet. 'They're private.'

A little shocked at the priest's temper, Bert immediately handed the books back.

'I'm sorry about your bicycle,' he said, looking down to the beach. The bike was missing a wheel.

'Hmpf,' said Father Hooper. 'You shouldn't have been lying across the path.' He peered over the cliff edge tentatively. 'That could have been me down there,' he said, turning green.

Bert tried to force the picture of Father Hooper sliding down the cliff face on his bottom out of his mind, when a shiny object, glinting in the sunlight, caught his eye. It was the priest's wire-rimmed spectacles resting on a piece of rock that jutted out from beneath the cliff edge. He bent down and, holding on to a gorse bush root, scooped them up in his hand – but as he turned round to offer them to Father Hooper, he saw the priest, his tunic covered in grass stains and his cape flapping behind him, scurrying over the tussock grass towards the old chapel. The ledgers were piled high in his arms.

'Your spectacles—' Bert shouted feebly, but the priest kept running. He examined the pair of glasses in his hand. They looked old, like no other glasses he'd seen, and both lenses were dusty. One of them was cracked. He licked his finger and smeared it round the lenses to clear off the film of dirt.

Strange man, he thought, and he set off to give them back.

According to the gaffer, the old chapel on the cliff path dated back to the thirteenth century. A small, dark building with stained-glass windows and a crooked bell tower, it was said to be the only mediaeval building left remaining after the area had been struck by a devastating fire. It was now only occasionally used for church services and most of the time its heavy oak door stood firmly locked. Clearing away a cobweb with his sleeve, Bert peered in through a small window. The chapel seemed dark and empty. Thinking that maybe the chaplain was still outside, Bert wandered around the building.

'Father Hooper?' he called.

A seagull sitting on the tiled roof picked at a fish carcass. It cawed at Bert, picked up its meal and flew off.

The ground around the chapel was uneven, and a few ancient gravestones littered the tussock grass. Bert stood on tiptoes and peered in through another window. Multicoloured shafts of sunlight fell across the pews and altar, but there still didn't seem to be signs of anyone in there. In fact it didn't look like there'd been anyone inside for years. Bert knocked on the window.

'Father Hooper?' he called again.

'Robert Twistleton,' came a chirpy voice.

Bert spun round, lost his footing and fell over. Rubbing his backside, he heard someone beside him giggling. He peered up, squinting into the sunlight. It was Ruby H-B.

'Are you all right, Robert?' she asked, trying to suppress a laugh.

'Fine, thanks,' said Bert curtly, obviously in some pain.

Ruby H-B was in the same class as Bert at school. H-B stood for Harrison-Burbett, or something like that. Bert had never really paid much attention. She was a bit of a teacher's pet.

'What were you doing?' she asked, trying to peer into the chapel.

'Looking for the priest,' said Bert, pulling the spectacles out of his back pocket. 'He dropped these on the cliff path.' Both lenses were now cracked. 'What are you doing round here?' he asked.

'My dad's on the beach with his silly metal detector,' said Ruby, fiddling with one of her auburn pigtails. Her dad worked in the hotel as a part-time maintenance engineer. 'I spotted you running along the cliff path.'

'Did you see Father Hooper?' asked Bert.

Ruby shook her head.

Bert tried to get up. 'Ow!' he yelped, clutching his leg. He must have twisted his ankle when he fell. Ruby put an arm around him and they hobbled to a fallen gravestone and sat down.

'I heard about your granny,' said Ruby as Bert rubbed his ankle. 'I'm sorry.'

Bert grunted.

'My dad says they still haven't found her yet. The whole village is going on about it.'

'I'd rather not talk about it, thanks,' said Bert. He still felt confused about the whole episode, and he certainly wasn't going to discuss it with a girl he hardly knew.

'Right,' said Ruby, slightly embarrassed.

'I ought to get back,' said Bert, trying to get up. 'Mum'll need a hand with lunch.'

'Yeah, my dad'll be wondering where I got to,' said

Ruby, looking about. 'This place gives me the creeps anyway.'

As Bert put his hand back to push himself up, the gravestone seemed to groan. Bert frowned. 'I don't think this thing is very stable,' he said.

Suddenly there was a terrific yawning, and the stone gave way beneath them.

'Hang on to something,' yelled Bert.

'Ahhh!' Ruby screamed, desperately trying to clutch on to the tussock grass around her.

Together they fell back, down into the darkness. With a heavy thud, they landed on a stone floor, cushioned by the earth and grass that had fallen with them.

'Crikey,' muttered Bert.

Ruby groaned as she sat up. 'Where are we?' she asked. 'Do you think . . . we're in someone's grave?'

Bert got up and hobbled around in the darkness. A weak shaft of light from the hole above revealed they were in a small stone room. The walls had writing upon them. A sort of graffiti, but not in English.

'Too big to be a grave, I think,' he said, his ankle still in some pain. 'More like some sort of vault.'

'How are we going to get out?' asked Ruby.

Bert looked up towards the surface. He could see the seagulls circling high above. 'If you got on my shoulders,' he said, 'you could get out and help me up.'

'Well, what are we waiting for?' said Ruby grumpily.

'Hang on a moment,' said Bert. 'I think I've found something.' In the darkness, he could feel a cold metal object protruding from the wall. 'I think it's a door,' he said. He gave it a yank. A chink of light appeared.

'What's a door doing down here?' asked Ruby.

'Search me,' said Bert. He gave it another pull. The hinges creaked as the door inched open.

Ruby peered through the opening. 'It's . . . a corridor,' she said, now whispering. 'And it's lit by candles.'

Bert pulled the door open further. They both stood looking down into the passageway. It seemed to stretch for about a hundred yards, with another smaller wooden door at the other end. The walls were made from jagged stone and there were ledges on either side with dozens of burning candles dripping wax on to the floor.

'Where do you think it leads to?' asked Ruby.

'Under the chapel,' said Bert quietly. 'I think I can hear voices.'

Ruby cupped her ear, her face contorted with concentration. The distinctive murmur of a conversation could be heard coming from the end of the corridor.

'I thought you said there wasn't any sign of anyone inside?' whispered Ruby angrily.

'There wasn't,' said Bert. He stepped into the light.

'Robert,' whispered Ruby sharply, 'I don't think you should go down there. We're not supposed to be here at all.'

'Come on,' said Bert.

'We shouldn't be doing this,' mumbled Ruby.

They tiptoed down the corridor, Ruby concentrating on the candles that were worryingly close to her hair. The voices were getting louder.

As Bert reached the small heavy door, he pressed his ear against it. 'I think it must be the vestry,' he whispered.

'Let me hear,' said Ruby.

Bert noticed a keyhole beneath the rusty door handle. He pulled the priest's spectacles out of his pocket, placed them on the ledge beside the door and squatted down.

'Missing? What do you mean they've gone missing?' came a deep voice from inside the vestry.

'Peculiar,' said Bert. 'That sounds like the gaffer.' He peered in through the keyhole. His grandfather and the priest were standing on the other side of the vestry door, surrounded by the thick brown ledgers that Bert had seen earlier.

'I've searched through all the records here and in the village church,' came the higher-pitched voice of Father Hooper, 'and this is all I managed to find.'

Bert's grandfather picked up one of the heavy

books and flicked through it. 'But these ledgers don't tell us anything,' he spat.

'Please keep your voice down, Godfrey,' said the priest frantically. 'Someone'll hear you.'

'Don't be so absurd, man,' blasted the gaffer. 'We're ten feet under ground.'

'One can't be too careful,' said the priest, plainly nervous. 'If anyone found out about this, there'd be hell to pay.'

Chapter Three

Tap tap tap

Bert rolled over and tried to get back to sleep. Getting up in the morning was not his forte.

Tap tap tap

He opened one eye. His bedroom was dark, with a chink of sunlight breaking through the curtains. Was someone knocking on the door or the window?

'I'm asleep!' he croaked. 'Go away,' and he stuck his head under the pillow.

Tap tap . . .

'Right, that does it,' he mumbled angrily. Pulling back the duvet, he swung his legs out of bed and launched himself at the door. It was then that he remembered his ankle from the afternoon before.

'ARGHH!' he yelped, hopping up and down. As he fell back on to his bed, the knocking came again. Someone was at his bedroom window. Bert leant over and pulled back the curtains. A shaft of light hit him straight in the face.

'Delivery for Mr Twistleton,' came a voice from outside. 'Mr Godfrey Twistleton.'

Bert looked at his watch. It was seven twenty-five in the morning.

'Try the front door!' he called, fighting to open the window.

'Front door's locked,' said the man.

Bert spotted the enormous wooden box in the back of the delivery van.

'OK,' he groaned, 'I'll come round.'

Bert hopped over to the chair in the corner of the room and pulled his jeans on over his boxer shorts. He kept the T-shirt on he'd slept in, a habit his mum found deeply repellent.

The apartment hallway was quiet, apart from the tinny sound of the Coldstream Guards Band playing in the bathroom. Bert's dad was obviously shaving. His mum would probably be through in the hotel by now, dealing with the kitchen staff as they prepared breakfast. Tallulah, Bert's younger sister, was probably still asleep.

Thwatthwat went the door as it bounced back on its sprung hinges.

The tiles of the mosaic floor were cold under Bert's feet. Crossing the giant lobby with a slight limp, he went to unbolt the main doors. Outside, the sun was shining and the delivery-man was waiting with the box loaded on to a trolley. He shoved a clipboard and pen in Bert's face. Bert signed it and the man dumped the box at his feet, then spun round and jogged back towards the van.

'Could we move it into the hallway?' Bert called after him.

But the man was already in the driver's seat. With a cough of diesel fumes, the van rumbled to life and sped off down the driveway.

'Excellent,' grumbled Bert, and he tried to lift the box. He needn't have bothered; whatever was in it weighed a ton. Looking forward to climbing back into bed, he pushed the box through the front doors into the hallway towards the Twistletons' apartment. It rattled as he edged it down the hall steps.

When he had eventually reached his grandfather's bedroom door, Bert leant forward to knock, but stopped. Would the gaffer be awake yet? Bert had never actually been inside his grandfather's room. He'd peeked in once, but only briefly. The door was almost always locked. He pressed his ear against it.

'Robert!' shrieked a voice from behind, making him jump so violently he banged his head on the door. 'What on earth do you think you're doing?'

It was Bert's mum, with a box of paper in her arms.

Her hair tied up in a towering beehive, she looked like she'd been up for hours.

'Golly. Morning. I was just delivering a box to Grandpa,' said Bert, embarrassed.

'You were eavesdropping, Robert,' said his mum. 'Your grandfather's been through quite enough recently. And why aren't you wearing any shoes?'

'Well, erm, you see, there was a delivery-man at my window and . . .'

'Is that the same T-shirt you slept in last night?'

'I was going to change it,' said Bert.

'That's revolting. There are clean T-shirts in your wardrobe. This is a hotel, Robert, not an orphanage.'

Mrs Twistleton headed towards the kitchen. Bert stuck his tongue out as she disappeared around the corner.

'And don't stick your tongue out, Robert,' she called.

Bert kicked the box and shuffled over to his bedroom door. As he went in he leapt on to his bed and closed his eyes. His ankle was throbbing even more now.

'Robert?' It was Bert's mum again. 'Don't go back to bed, I need some help.'

Bert groaned. It was just going to be one of those days. He pulled on his trainers, still caked in mud from the graveyard, and hobbled out into the hall. He noticed the box outside his grandfather's room had now disappeared.

The kitchen was starting to fill up with members of the hotel staff.

'Morning, Robert,' called Mr Dawbany, the children's entertainer, in his thick Cornish accent.

Robert wasn't used to seeing Mr Dawbany in his everyday clothes. He normally wandered around the ground floor of the hotel saving the world in a tight leotard and cape, dressed as his alter ego 'Captain Fabulous'. 'Elvis the Wonder Dog', his pet pug that looked as though he'd had a nasty accident with a brick wall, cowered under the kitchen table.

Behind Bert a number of the other usual suspects filtered in: Aurelia and Alveria, the Spanish cooks; Mrs Gubbins, the head of the laundry staff; and Mr H-B, the part-time maintenance engineer and father of Ruby. Finally, as Bert's mum organized her papers at the head of the kitchen table, Mr Whicker appeared, miaowing as he shuffled across the room. Elvis the pug dog growled under the table.

'Robert, hand these out,' said Bert's mum, pushing the papers towards him. Each duplicated sheet had a title and a numbered list beneath it, and at the bottom, in bold letters, it read, 'Printed by the Whicker Grocery Press'.

Bert's mum cleared her throat.

'Good morning, ladies and gentlemen,' she began. Captain Fabulous yawned, peered at his watch and closed his eyes. 'I've called you all to this rather early morning meeting to discuss the plans for the major event of this year's holiday season calendar.'

Mr Dawbany had started to snore.

'THE SOLAR ECLIPSE!' shouted Bert's mum and she banged her fist down on to the table.

Mr Dawbany almost fell off his chair.

'As you know, we have been planning for this moment for some time. And, if our pre-bookings are to be realized, this shall be the busiest weekend in the hotel's entire history.'

Bert's mum beamed with pride. Dawbany began to yawn again.

'With only three days until the event, the hotel is already bursting with guests. The kitchen has taken on extra staff, and Mr Tuttle from the village joinery has kindly offered to provide us with further beds should we need them.'

As his mother broke into full flow, Bert manoeuvred his way round the room handing out the leaflets. And as he placed the leftover sheets back on the table, he dropped one. Ducking down to pick it up, he came face to face with Elvis, who was busy cocking his leg over Mr Whicker's shoe.

'Dear God!' yelped Mr Whicker suddenly, leaping away from the table. 'What the hell has your vermin mutt done on my leg?'

Bert shut his eyes.

'Elvis?' hollered Captain Fabulous, suddenly waking up. 'My Elvis isn't vermin!'

'YOUR FLIPPING ELVIS HAS JUST PEED ON MY SHOE!' yelled Whicker, his voice quivering.

'Quiet, gentlemen, this is a staff meeting,' called Bert's mum, trying to calm everyone down. 'Now, where was I?'

'But Captain Calamity's dog's a ruddy health hazard!'

'How dare you call me Captain Calamity!' and with that Mr Dawbany swung a punch at the grocer. Whicker ducked, and Mrs Gubbins caught Dawbany's punch straight in the face.

'Gentlemen. Gentlemen, please,' called out Mrs Twistleton. 'Quiet. PLEASE!'

Bert began to back out of the room while Mr Whicker and Captain Fabulous chased each other around the kitchen table.

'Order, gentleman,' cried Bert's mum. 'ORDER!'

And then, as if the morning hadn't started strangely enough, Bert thought he caught the sound of a revving engine coming from behind him. There was a distinct smell of exhaust fumes too. He looked about. The hallway was empty. He realized the sound and smell were coming from his grandfather's room. As he walked over and pressed his ear against the door, there was an enormous *BOOM*, and the gaffer's door flew open and knocked Bert flying.

'YEEEHAAAAA!' came a cry that sounded distinctly like the gaffer.

The chaos in the kitchen was stunned into silence

as from out of the bedroom rode Bert's grandfather upon a small and very peculiar-looking moped. He was wearing a pair of flying goggles, a long white lab coat, and a pair of gardening gloves. As he circled the hallway to the guffaws of the hotel staff, Bert's grandpa yanked a lever and a number of mechanical arms sprung out from under the seat and started to brush and polish the stone floor around him.

'Behold!' cried the gaffer, delighted by the attention of his captive audience. 'My newest invention. The world's first motorized cleaning and polishing cycle, perfect for use indoors and out!'

There was a loud belch and a cloud of foul-smelling green gas erupted from the moped's exhaust pipe.

'And it's entirely powered by seaweed!' cried the gaffer over the noise. 'So no horrid engine smells.'

Bert watched in stunned amazement as the speechless crowd spilled out from the kitchen into the hall. Apart from the priest, no one had really seen the gaffer since his wife's mysterious disappearance.

In a blaze of flashing lights and with sirens wailing, the gaffer rode the machine down the corridor towards the hotel lobby.

'Come and see how my newest brainwave, only recently back from rigorous testing on the continent, will save hours of backbreaking housework.'

The moped farted again, and with a *thwatthwat*

disappeared from view. Bert watched, mesmerized, as the crowd followed the inventor out through the lobby door as if he was the Pied Piper of Hamelin. In a matter of seconds the apartment was empty, apart from Elvis the rabid pug dog, who was now shredding Mr Whicker's shoe under the kitchen table.

As Bert sat on the cold stone floor, still a little shaken from being knocked off his feet, it slowly dawned upon him that his grandfather's door was standing wide open in front of him. Everyone had gone, and they were likely to be gone for some time. His curiosity getting the better of him, Bert crawled towards the door and peered into the bedroom. It was not what he had expected at all. Everything was in its rightful place, with the large wooden bed over by the far wall, a wardrobe, a chest of drawers with a pile of jumpers folded neatly on top of it, a sink in the corner and a beautiful Persian rug laid out over the floorboards on the ground. But there was no sign of the wooden box which, Bert presumed, had contained the parts for the moped.

And then Bert spotted the ledgers on his grandfather's bedside table. There were eight of them piled high, the same ones he'd seen with the priest on the cliff path and in the vestry. Getting up, he tiptoed over, slid one off the pile and went to sit on the tiny chair beside his grandfather's bed to read it. But just as he put his weight on the cushioned seat, the chair collapsed beneath him. It didn't break; it just sank quite slowly down into the ground. And as the chair went down, to Bert's astonishment a small gap in the far wall opened up.

Bert blinked for a moment. Fighting to get up, he took his weight off the chair, and immediately it rose again. And as the chair rose, the doorway in the far wall closed. Bert was quite gobsmacked. Nothing like this had ever happened in the hotel before, and he'd lived there all his life. He sat down to think, and as he sat, he sank and the doorway silently appeared before him again.

Leaning over, Bert slid the ledgers one by one off the table beside him and placed them on to the seat underneath his bottom. This time as he got up, the chair stayed down, and with the door in the wall remaining open, he crept across the room.

'Hello?' he called.

The doorway opened up into a small corridor that disappeared into darkness. Bert checked the hallway behind him. There was nobody about, and he could still hear the noise of the moped roaring around the hotel lobby. He peered back into the darkness. He wasn't usually the type to creep down dark alleyways, and this was the second he'd found in two days.

'Is anybody there?' he called.

Silence.

Bert felt the jagged stone walls for a light switch. No luck. Slowly, quietly and listening out for the return of anyone to the apartment, Bert made his way down the corridor. It didn't go far. At its end the corridor opened up into a large room. Again he felt for a light switch. This time he found a cord, and as he tugged it, four torches hanging on the walls burst into flame. Bert's jaw dropped at what he found.

The room was square, with a ceiling held up by four huge pillars. Plan chests overflowing with paper hugged the walls, and blueprints, huge maps, and drawings littered the stone floor.

Tentatively, Bert stepped into the room and picked up one of the plans. It showed the details of a tunnel system, a labyrinth of rooms and old sewers. There were strange words scrawled across it, written in a language Bert didn't recognize, like the writing in the vault. He recognized the cliff line as the headland outside.

But if that was the case, he thought, then beneath the hotel, beneath where he was standing, the ground was a warren of passages and rooms. He picked up another map, this one with a huge wax seal at the bottom with the shape of a cross pressed into it. It was definitely the Baloddan area, with individual houses highlighted. If these maps were real, then the whole village was built upon a maze of tunnels that wound their way around the area like an underground road system. But in the eleven years of his life Bert had heard nothing of them, which meant surely, that no one else knew of them either. Apart from the gaffer...

Bert was confused enough, when suddenly he noticed the walls around him. Hundreds and hundreds of photographs of different sizes decorated every inch of stone. There were family holiday snaps, photos torn from newspapers and even the odd passport shot. Some of the pictures were obviously portions of a much larger original. In each case, one person was highlighted, often with a ring drawn around the individual's face. Beside each picture was a date written in the gaffer's distinctive handwriting. Bert leant closer to read one of them.

'Felicity Redmond. Disappeared February 1943. Age 85. Baloddan Library, presumed eaten.'

Bert rubbed his eyes and read it again. Eaten? Surely this was some sort of joke. He read another one.

'Albemarle Jessop. Died December 1928. 85 yrs. Spontaneous Human Combustion, public toilets.'

Bert thought he was going mad. He pulled down a photograph. It looked such a normal, happy scene: a red-haired lady holding a cooing child. The other photos were similar. There were postmen on their bikes, trawler men in their boats, laughing mothers with their children, and all seemingly local to Baloddan. But each photo seemed to record a strange death or disappearance that went back years.

1897 was the earliest Bert could find with a photograph. But that had turned all brown and the edges were curling. Some dates went back even further without any pictures beside them at all.

'Brother John Vernon 1687, in the reign of King James the second, during matins.'

On the far wall there was one photograph set aside from the rest. Bert didn't need to read the caption to know who it was. It was his grandmother.

Suddenly Bert heard the familiar *thwatthwat* and the sound of the moped engine entering the apartment. He'd be mincemeat if he was caught in his grandfather's room, and he rushed to leave. He pulled the light cord and shoved the photo of the red-haired lady into his trouser pocket. In a flash, Bert was back out into the gaffer's room, heaping the books back on to the bedside table.

'Robert?' came Bert's grandfather's voice. 'Is that you in there?'

Slowly the opening in the wall closed as the chair rose up from the floor. Bert's grandpa walked into the room, with his goggles and helmet under his arm, just as the gap in the wall disappeared.

'Grandpa!' said Bert, feigning surprise at the sight of the gaffer.

'What are you doing in here, Robert?' asked the gaffer. 'You shouldn't enter people's rooms unless you've been invited.'

'Ah yes, I'm sorry,' stuttered Bert. 'I found the

door open and was just closing it when I saw these extraordinary books.'

Bert was trying to make his way towards the door.

'Amazing. I couldn't put this one down,' said Bert. 'Fascinating writer.'

Bert thought he was doing well. His grandfather watched him cross the room.

'Well,' said Bert, 'I'd better be off.'

He handed the last book back to his grandfather, but let go a moment too early. The book fell to the ground with a loud thud, the pages flapping open. Each page was totally clear of writing. The book was empty.

Bert and his grandfather stared at each other for a second.

'I think you should leave,' said the gaffer slowly. Bert stepped into the hallway and his grandfather closed the door behind him.

Chapter Four

Bert had never really been into superheroes. He'd always thought Clark Kent looked a bit daft dressed up in his shiny Superman outfit. And anyone who wore sparkly pants that tight had to be very strange indeed.

There were some superheroes, however, that pushed the boundaries of tasteful outfits to the very limit. Mr Dawbany, the Baloddan Hotel's very own 'Captain Fabulous', was one of them.

'All right, children, gather round,' called Mr Dawbany, his leotard more resembling an overweight wrestler's than a superhero's.

Fifty or so children, all dressed in shorts and

T-shirts, huddled around the entertainer. He handed a sheet of paper, a clipboard and a packed lunch to each outstretched hand. Bert remained seated on the hall staircase, where he watched in silence.

'Today's activities will kick off with a crazy golf competition, followed by an athletics afternoon down on the beach.'

The children cooed with anticipation while Miss Crankshaft, the aerobics instructor, handed out badges to each contestant.

Bert looked at his watch. Eleven twenty-seven. His granny's memorial service at the old chapel would be starting any moment. He leant over and shined his shoe with his jacket sleeve. He felt a bit silly wearing a sports jacket and tie. Where *had* his grandfather got to?

'Have we got everybody, Miss Crankshaft?' chirped the caped crusader. The instructor, already jogging on the spot, nodded.

'This way then,' and the team of crazy golfers were led through the hotel front doors, their flip-flops clipping over the colourful harbour scene tiled on the hallway floor.

As Bert watched Elvis trot after the lunch bags, he suddenly remembered the photograph he'd shoved into his trouser pocket the morning before. Pulling the now crumpled picture out, he studied the face of the beautiful young woman with freckles and red hair. Bert thought she looked a little familiar, and on turning it over was shocked to find her name, 'Marcie Harrison-Burbett'. That was Ruby's surname. They must be related, he thought. He looked at his watch again; where *had* the gaffer got to?

'Good morning, Robert,' came a shrill voice from the staircase above him. Bert spun round to find three large elderly women, all wearing gaudy bathing costumes, towels and tight rubber swimming caps, bearing down on him. He jumped up immediately.

'How wonderful to see you, Robert,' clucked one of the ladies. 'Haven't you grown since we last saw you?'

It was the Heaver sisters, three wobbling spinsters, probably in their late seventies, who'd been visiting the hotel each summer for the past forty years. One of them was holding a paper bag full of sweets.

'You *are* looking smart this morning, Robert,' said one of the ladies, patting Bert on the head. 'Anything we should know about?'

'Granny's memorial,' said Bert, squashing the photo back into his trouser pocket. 'Mum's asked me to escort my grandfather.'

'Ah, yes,' said one sister, her face contorting as she chewed on a toffee. 'Poor Godfrey. He must be devastated.'

'Awfully sad,' said another, straightening her towel.

'Have they actually found her body yet?' asked the third.

'Mildred!' gasped the other two, flapping their arms like a pair of alarmed chickens.

Bert sat down. 'No, they haven't,' he said. 'Not yet.'

Suddenly there was a large explosion and out through the apartment door sailed Bert's grandfather on his motorbike. The old ladies reeled back in horror as a cloud of green smoke belched from the machine's exhaust. The gaffer pulled up at the bottom of the stairs and lifted his goggles.

'Morning, ladies,' he shouted over the noise of the engine. The women stared at him in total shock. The gaffer handed Bert a pair of goggles and an old leather flying-hat. 'Come along, Robert,' he said. 'We'll be late for your grandmother's service.'

Bert climbed on to the seat behind his grandfather and wrapped his arms around him. With another cough, a cloud of green smoke spewed from the exhaust pipe, and Bert and the gaffer circled the hotel hallway.

'Tallyho!' shouted the gaffer at the gobsmacked ladies, and he and Bert rode straight through the open hallway doors and out into the sunshine.

'Well I never,' choked one of the Heaver sisters, frantically waving her arms to try to get rid of the smoke. The others weren't listening, however. They'd both fainted on the staircase.

The motorbike bounced over the lawn towards the cliff edge, leaving the vast hotel and crazy golf course behind. The gaffer twisted round and looked at Bert huddled on the seat behind him, with the sun on his face and the wind blowing his tie over his shoulder.

'We're going to take the cliff path,' said the gaffer. 'It'll be quicker.'

Bert nodded, and gripped on to his grandfather tightly. Leaning out slightly, he could see over the cliff edge and down far below to the crowd of tourists with their multicoloured windbreaks on the beach. The sand stretched for over a mile and a half, so Bert often wondered why the hotel guests never ventured more than a hundred yards from the cliff steps.

As the bike bounced over the uneven path, and the chinstraps on the gaffer's leather cap flapped behind his head like a dog's ears, Bert's mind wandered back to the awkward meeting in his grandfather's bedroom. The subject hadn't been spoken of again, and Bert was happy not to bring it up. For once, he was pleased that the moped engine made such a deafening noise.

The old chapel quickly grew closer until finally the gaffer was weaving the moped through the yew trees that surrounded the graveyard. He turned off the ignition and the bike rolled silently towards the porch for the last ten yards. The organ could be heard playing inside when they came to a halt directly outside the entrance. Bert hopped off and handed the hat and goggles to his grandfather.

'Thank you,' he said. 'For the lift.'

The gaffer leant the motorbike against the chapel wall, next to Father Hooper's one-wheeled bicycle. He knelt down and adjusted Bert's tie. Looking into Bert's eyes, he smiled.

'Ready?' he asked.

Bert straightened his back and nodded.

'Good,' and with his arm around his grandson, the gaffer led the way in through the seldom opened, heavy oak doors. Inside, the small, musty chapel was full, and the whole congregation turned to watch as Bert and his grandfather made their way down the central aisle, walking in time to the organ music being played by Mr Tuttle. Bert thought he recognized most of the mourners: the policeman with the hair growing out of his nose, the bent over and quietly miaowing Mr Whicker, the chattering ladies from the post office and a handful of off-duty staff from the hotel. In the front pew sat Bert's mum and dad, and his sister, Tallulah.

'You're late,' Tallulah hissed through her teeth as Bert squeezed in beside her.

'I had to wait for Grandpa,' said Bert. 'We got here on his new motorbike.'

Tallulah tutted into her service book.

'Dearly beloved,' the priest began from up in front of the altar. His nose still looked inflamed and the red blotches hadn't quite disappeared from his face. He was also wearing his spectacles, Bert noticed, with both lenses fixed.

'Psst,' came a whisper from behind him as Hooper was getting into full flow. Bert turned round. Ruby was standing directly behind him. She smiled. 'How's your ankle?' she mouthed.

'Better, thanks,' he said. He felt the photograph in his pocket. 'I've got something to show you . . .' he whispered.

'Shhhhh!' rasped Tallulah.

The priest glared at Bert. Bert turned puce.

The service went on for only half an hour. Without a body or a coffin, they didn't have anyone to bury, so once the last hymn had been sung, and the blessing had been said, everyone filed out into the sunshine. Bert made a beeline straight for Ruby.

'I need to talk to you,' he said, checking his grandfather wasn't within hearing distance.

Ruby looked intrigued. 'Is it about what we found the other day?' she asked. 'I haven't said a word to anyone.'

Bert looked round. The priest was shaking hands with his dad.

'Not really,' said Bert. 'Well, sort of. It might be. I don't know.'

He led Ruby away from the gathering.

'I found *another* hidden room,' he said.

Ruby stared at him. 'Go on,' she said.

'It's in the hotel, next to my grandfather's room,' whispered Bert. 'It had a hidden door, and inside there were maps and plans of hundreds of tunnels that lead between here and the village.'

'Your grandfather's been digging tunnels?' asked Ruby, a little confused.

'No, I don't think so,' said Bert. 'I think they're hundreds of years old, but he definitely knows something about them. And there were all these photographs stuck to the walls.' He pulled the crumpled picture out of his back trouser pocket, and handed it to Ruby.

'That's my Aunt Marcie,' she said frowning.

'That *was* your Aunt Marcie, don't you mean?' asked Bert. He turned the picture over, and pointed to his grandfather's inscription on the back. 'Spontaneous Human Combustion, Hotel laundry, 2 November 1972. She's dead, isn't she?'

Ruby looked puzzled. 'I don't think so,' she said, turning Bert around. 'She's talking to your mother.'

Bert almost choked. The woman in the photograph, although now looking older, was indeed having an animated conversation with his mum, over a cup of tea and a custard cream.

'But, but, but . . . this can't be right,' he spluttered. 'Her photo was on the wall, with lots of other dead people. My grandmother's was up there,' said Bert, 'and *she's* dead.'

'I hope she is,' said Ruby, feigning a smile at her aunt who'd now been joined by the priest, 'we've just had her memorial service.'

'Something very strange is going on here,' said Bert gravely, studying the picture.

'You bet it is,' said Ruby. 'I've known my aunt all my life, and now you're telling me she's supposed to be dead?'

But Bert didn't answer. He was deep in thought. 'We need to find out what's going on. Where can we find the public records from 1972?' he asked.

'I beg your pardon?' asked Ruby.

'According to my grandfather's writing, your aunt disappeared in November 1972, in the laundry of the hotel, right?' said Bert.

'But it's plainly wrong,' said Ruby. 'Look, why don't we just go and ask your grandfather what it's all about?'

Bert glanced over at the gaffer kneeling in the grass as he studied the floral tributes laid below the chapel windows. 'I don't think we should bother him right now,' he said. 'Let's try the records first. If she *did* pass away, it *would* be recorded, right?'

Ruby sighed heavily. 'I guess,' she said.

'And *if* she's alive, then we *won't* find her name, will we?'

'No,' said Ruby.

'OK then,' said Bert. 'And if your aunt's alive, then maybe my grandmother is too. So let's find those records.'

Suddenly Ruby guessed where the conversation was leading.

'I'm not stepping foot in that vestry for anyone,' she whispered.

Bert took Ruby's arm and smiled.

'Oh yes, you are,' he said.

Bert led Ruby through the small crowd to the chapel porch. He saw that the grave they'd fallen down a couple of days before had been repaired, and a bunch of flowers had been placed on the headstone.

'Someone'll see us if we go back inside,' whispered Ruby.

But no one seemed in the least bit concerned. Bert's grandfather was talking to the hairy police officer and the priest was making his way over to Mrs Gubbins, who was handing out her home-made fruitcake. Bert pulled Ruby in through the doors.

'This is a bad idea, Robert Twistleton,' said Ruby, checking to see if they were alone. 'If we get caught, I'm blaming it all on you.'

'Afternoon!' called a chirpy voice from up near the altar.

Bert spun round to find Mr Tuttle the organ player walking quickly towards them with his music books under one arm. His rubber-soled shoes squeaked as he hurried down the aisle.

'Come back inside for a bit of peace and quiet?' he asked.

Bert and Ruby nodded.

'Well, I'll leave you to it,' he said, pulling open the door. 'Don't want to miss the cake.'

Ruby forced a smile, and Mr Tuttle disappeared into the sunshine. As the door closed again Ruby let out her breath.

'Come on,' said Bert. 'The entrance must be up here.'

They both walked quickly up to the east end of the church, and as they climbed the few steps that led to the choir stalls they spotted a small, arched door beneath the organ pipes.

'That must be it,' said Bert.

'I hope it's locked,' said Ruby.

Bert tried the handle, and with a heave the door slowly opened towards them.

'Just my luck,' whispered Ruby.

On the other side of the doorway was a spiral stone staircase.

'Well, that must be the way to the tower,' he said looking up, 'and the vestry must be down below.'

He began to descend the stairs. Ruby didn't move.

'Well, come along,' said Bert anxiously. 'We don't have all day.'

Ruby stepped through and swung the door closed behind her. It shut with a loud bang. Bert froze.

'Sorry,' she whispered.

The dark staircase was lit by thin shafts of daylight that streamed in through narrow slits in the walls. At the base of the steps the windows were filled in, and a single flickering candle lodged in a nook in the wall lit another, even smaller, arched door in front of them.

'This must be it,' said Bert.

'Are you sure we want to do this?' asked Ruby, but Bert had already turned the handle.

The room on the other side was totally dark. Bert felt for a light switch and clicked it on. As soon as he did though, he wished he'd stayed out in the sunshine.

'Oh my goodness,' whispered Ruby.

The vestry had been ransacked. The table in the centre of the small, dimly lit room had been turned over and there were sheets of paper and old hymn-books scattered across the floor. Drawers had been pulled out of chests and emptied, and pictures had been knocked from the walls. A stale, musty smell that smelt oddly familiar to Bert hung in the air. Almost like the cat litter tray outside the hotel apartment's back door.

'It looks as though we're not the only ones searching for something,' said Bert, stepping inside.

Ruby stayed outside the door. 'I don't like it down here,' she said. 'I think we should leave.'

'Let's find what we came for and then go,' said Bert, reaching for one of the books that lay scattered on the floor in front of him. Flipping the cover open, he found it was a chronological list of every person who'd lived in the parish in the 1950s. Ruby, meanwhile, tentatively stepped over a bench lying across the floor and peered into an empty filing cabinet.

'Well, *I* think this is pointless,' she said.

'Nonsense,' said Bert, standing up. He moved across the room and picked up another book. 'I've found something already. "Births and deaths, Baloddan Parish, 1970 to 1979." ' Perching on the side of a moth-eaten armchair, he shook the dust off the book and opened the front cover. 'Hmmm. Nineteen seventy, seventy-one.' He flicked through the pages. 'Seventy-two . . . November.' He moved his finger down the long list of names. 'Right. Hamish, Hardy, Harrelson, Heddington. Oh,' he said as his finger reached the bottom of the page. 'Well, no H-B in here.'

He turned to face Ruby only to find she was no longer standing beside him. She was the other side of the room with her head stuck in an open safe. 'Your aunt's not in the book,' he called. 'She seems to be very much alive.'

'Right. Good,' replied Ruby. 'I mean, I thought she must have been.'

Bert stumbled over to join her. 'What are you doing?' he asked. 'Have you found something?'

'Just a silly old safe,' said Ruby. 'Practically empty.'

'Practically?' asked Bert.

'Well . . . you know those tunnel maps you mentioned?'

'The ones I found with that photograph?' said Bert.

'Yes, well did any of them have a large wax seal in a bottom corner?'

Bert thought for a second. 'Yes. One had a cross pressed into it. Why?'

Ruby turned round. In her hands was a map, very similar to the two Bert had found the day before. Her map had a seal in the bottom corner too.

'More tunnels?' asked Bert.

'I think so,' said Ruby. 'And what's more, I think I've just found out who made that wax seal. From behind her back Ruby produced a heavy metal stamp with a large cross embossed on the bottom of it. She also had half a melted wax stick in her hand.

'Father Hooper?' said Bert, rather astonished. 'Are we the only ones who *don't* know about these tunnels?'

Suddenly the door up in the chapel banged closed, and footsteps echoed on the stone staircase.

'Someone's coming,' said Bert.

'What are we going to do?' whispered Ruby, starting to panic.

'Hide!'

Ruby shoved the stamp and the wax back in the safe.

'Where's the door we found the other day?'

'It must be over here somewhere,' said Ruby, searching the walls for a handle.

'The keyhole faced the desk,' said Bert, feeling around the walls.

'It's not here,' said Ruby, as the footsteps on the staircase grew louder.

'It's got to be,' said Bert. 'It must be here somewhere. We must find it, Ruby!'

But Ruby had stopped looking.

'Robert,' she said slowly.

Bert spun round. The priest, ominous in his flowing black tunic, was standing in the doorway staring at them.

'Looking for something?' he asked.

Chapter Five

The springs of the old leather sofa that lived in Bert's father's office were so worn and soft that, once anyone sat down, there was a real fear the sofa would entirely engulf them. So as Bert and Ruby sat there in silence on the afternoon of Mrs Twistleton's memorial service, they both looked as small and uncomfortable as they plainly felt.

'So you're still denying that you ransacked the chapel vestry?' asked the priest, eyeballing Bert. 'Even though I caught you redhanded?'

'That's right,' said Bert. 'The vestry was in that state when we found it.'

The priest turned to face the window. Dark

storm clouds were brewing out to sea.

'Well, I don't believe you,' he said, cracking his knuckles behind his back. 'You're both lying.'

'How dare you call my daughter a *liar*,' blasted Mr H-B from the armchair on the other side of the room. 'My daughter would never be involved in such vandalism.'

Father Hooper began to laugh. A deep, hoarse laugh that made Bert shiver.

'Oh, I never said it was *vandalism*, Mr Harrison-Burbett,' said the priest. 'No, your daughter and the young Mr Twistleton here were looking for something specific.' He spun round and glared at Ruby and Bert. 'Tell us what you were looking for,' he spat.

Ruby had turned white as a sheet. 'Erm, well, Robert had come across a photograph—'

'We were looking for nothing,' Bert interrupted. 'We were just poking about, exploring, and we found ourselves down in the vestry.'

'Which just so happened to have been turned over?' blasted the priest.

'Yes,' said Bert.

Bert's father stood up from behind his desk. 'Do we really need to keep going through this, Father Hooper?' he asked. 'Robert and Ruby have told us they didn't do it, and I see no reason not to believe them.'

'They were up to something, I tell you,' said Hooper. 'You mark my words.'

Bert's father let out a sign. 'Robert, Ruby, it's time you left us,' he said, motioning towards the door. 'I think this is something you should let us sort out.'

Bert climbed to his feet and turned towards the door. Suddenly the priest grabbed his arm, bent down and stared at him straight in the face. Bert could smell his foul breath.

'Don't think you've got away with this,' said the priest in a low menacing whisper. 'I know who you are.'

Bert's father had opened the door. 'Come on,' he said. 'This way.'

'Ruby, I'll see you at home,' said her father.

Ruby smiled weakly at her dad and she and Bert made their way out into the hotel hallway. The door was quickly closed behind them.

Bert leant against the wall and slid down to the floor. 'Thank goodness that's over,' he sighed.

'I told you we'd get caught,' said Ruby crossly, 'but oh no, you chose to ignore me.'

'I didn't *force* you to come with me.'

Ruby sat down beside him. 'What did Hooper mean "I know who you are"?' she asked.

Bert thought for a moment. 'Search me,' he said, shrugging his shoulders. 'That priest's weird.'

Ruby nodded.

'Lucky we didn't actually take anything,' said Bert, 'otherwise we'd have been in real trouble.'

'Ah,' said Ruby. 'That's not entirely true.'

Bert looked up to find Ruby pulling the tunnel map from under her jumper. 'You stole the map?' he spluttered. 'Have you gone completely mad?'

'I'd meant to put it back,' said Ruby. 'It's just . . .'

'It's just what?'

'Well . . . you know that strange picture you found of my Aunt Marcie?'

Bert pulled the photo out of his back pocket.

'Right. Although we know she's not really . . . *dead*,' said Ruby, examining the back of the shot, 'it does mention that whatever *did* happen, happened in the laundry.'

'Right. And?'

'Well, according to this map,' said Ruby, scanning the parchment in front of her, 'there's a tunnel entrance that's located in that very same room.' She marked the spot with her finger.

'What are you suggesting?' asked Bert.

'Well, it wouldn't hurt to have a look, that's all.'

'You must be kidding,' exclaimed Bert, climbing to his feet. 'That old laundry's in the lower basements. They're even more out of bounds than Hooper's stupid vestry.'

'So who's the coward now?' asked Ruby smugly.

'OK, you want to go right this minute?' asked Bert, trying to call her bluff.

'All right.'

'Fine. What about your dad, he said he'd meet you at home?'

Ruby listened against the door. 'Oh, I think they'll be some time,' she said.

'We'll need some stuff of course. A torch and things,' said Bert. 'The electricity got turned off down there years ago. It'll be pitch black.'

'Fine with me,' said Ruby.

As they made their way across the hall towards the private apartment, the three Heaver sisters wobbled in through the hotel front doors. Still wearing their bathing costumes and hats, they were covered in sand and appeared a little out of breath.

'Phew! That weather's certainly turning,' said one of the ladies, rubbing her arms. 'Time for a warm shower, I think.'

'Ooh look, there's that darling Robert,' said the second. 'I wonder how his grandmother's memorial went?'

'Cooee!' called the third sister, chewing a toffee. 'Robert, darling.'

'Oh, not again,' said Bert, grabbing Ruby by the hand. 'Quick!'

They both ran for the door. *Thwatthwat* it went as it bounced back on its sprung hinges. The ladies stood there, a little astonished.

'Strange boy,' they said in unison, and they turned to climb the stairs.

There were several entrances to the basements, but the one most commonly used was in the Twistleton apartment. A worn, granite staircase led down from the hall, and as Ruby stared into the darkness she began to have second thoughts about agreeing to accompany Bert.

'It *does* look a bit dark down there,' she said, shining the torch Bert had found under the kitchen sink.

'Don't be daft,' said Bert, and he flicked a light switch at the top of the steps. 'The first basement's lit, it's the floor underneath that's not.'

'Right,' said Ruby curtly, clicking off the spot light, and she started to descend the staircase.

'I take it you know where we're going?' she called.

'Shhh,' said Bert, taking the torch from her. 'Keep your voice down. We don't want the whole world knowing what we're up to.'

At the base of the stairwell a doorway opened up into a small, dimly lit room from where dozens of dingy corridors spread out in all directions like fingers from a hand. Huge stone slabs lined the floor, and condensation dripped on to them from the lead pipes that criss-crossed the ceiling.

'This place is a labyrinth,' exclaimed Ruby.

'Just mind your head,' said Bert. 'Dad's got countless scars from where he's whacked himself on the hotel plumbing system.'

Ruby took out the map and studied it. 'OK. How do we get down to the laundry rooms?' she asked.

'Well, I haven't been down there before, but I think I know where the staircase is.'

Bert led Ruby along a thin passageway. The old ceiling lights buzzed and flickered above their heads.

'These corridors were used by the room maids for years,' said Bert, ducking under a pipe. 'It meant they could hurry about the hotel without getting under the guests' feet.'

'Right,' said Ruby, starting to feel the cold.

'There are dozens of staff staircases that make their way up to each floor,' he said, passing another stairwell. 'They exit out through doors made to look like linen cupboards. Clever, hey?'

'Very,' said Ruby, checking that nobody was following them. 'Can we move a bit quicker?'

Finally they reached the end of the winding corridor where an old wooden dresser stood against the wall.

'This is it,' said Bert.

'You are joking, aren't you?' asked Ruby.

'I thought you were supposed to be clever?' said Bert sarcastically. 'It's *behind* the dresser. This is to stop anyone going down there. For their own safety apparently.'

Bert opened one of the drawers, grabbed the dresser's wooden frame, and heaved the piece of furniture towards him. 'Come on,' he strained, 'give me a hand.'

'It's a bit dirty,' said Ruby.

Slowly the huge piece of furniture slid out towards them. Ruby peered behind it, and was met by a solid, new-looking wall.

'Well, the staircase *may* have been here once upon a time, but it's been bricked up.'

'Oh,' said Bert, a little surprised.

'Well, maybe it was a foolish idea anyway,' said Ruby. 'Let's call it a day.'

'Not so fast,' replied Bert. 'There might be one other way of getting down there.'

'And that is?'

'The service lift,' said Bert, leading the way back down the gloomy corridor. 'The lift is still occasionally used to get to this level, but the shaft must go all the way down.'

They wound their way back into the first room, and took another of the corridors that led to a larger, square room with a lift shaft in the centre. Bars and a heavy metal gate prevented anyone falling down into the massive hole that dropped into the abyss.

'Well, here we are,' said Bert, pressing the 'call lift' button.

For a second nothing happened, and then a loud groan echoed from out of the darkness as the lift, somewhere high up in the hotel, descended to the first basement.

'It can be a little temperamental,' shouted Bert over the din. 'It's a—'

'Hammerstein 35 dual wheel chain elevator,' said

Ruby. 'Probably built in the early 1920s.'

'I beg your pardon?' asked Bert, almost choking.

Ruby blushed. 'Just a hobby,' she said.

Bert was speechless.

'All right, my dad's a bit of a lift nut. I just kind of picked a few things up.'

'You really are a swot, aren't you?' said Bert as the lift arrived.

He swung open the gate and pulled the concertina door open. The lift bounced a bit as he stepped in.

'Ready?' he asked, switching on the torch.

Ruby took a deep breath and tentatively stepped inside. 'I think so,' she said.

With a terrific grating rattle, Bert heaved the door closed and pressed the descend button.

'Going down,' he called, and the lift dropped out of sight.

As the metal cage plunged deep beneath the hotel, the glow from the first basement above became weaker and weaker until finally the only source of light was the dim glow from Bert's torch. He tapped it against the metal bars to try to make it shine brighter.

'Stupid thing,' he muttered.

'Robert?' said Ruby. 'You know you said you'd never been down to the lower basements before?'

'Yes,' said Bert. 'My father says it isn't safe enough. A bit of a maze apparently.'

'Well, how do we find the laundry when we get down there?'

'Hmm, good point.'

'And then once we *do* find it, how do we find our way back?'

'Hadn't thought of that either,' said Bert. 'We'll just have to remember every turn we take. It shouldn't be too difficult.'

Suddenly the lift jolted violently as it reached the second basement. Bert pulled the lift door open and pushed open the gate. They were faced with complete darkness.

'Crikey, it's cold,' said Ruby, flapping her arms.

Bert shonc his torch out in front of them. The walls of a large room were just visible in the gloom.

'It doesn't look like there's been anyone down here for years,' whispered Ruby.

'The new laundry upstairs was finished just after I was born,' said Bert.

They both stepped out of the lift. Bert swung the torch beam around the room. Again various corridors led off in different directions.

'Which way?' asked Ruby, holding tightly on to Bert's arm.

'Let's try this one,' he said in his most confident voice.

Slowly they made their way down a narrow passageway. Bert shone the flashlight into each room they passed.

'I suppose we're looking for old washing machines or clothes lines,' said Ruby.

Rounding a corner, they came into another opening, where a huge stone staircase rose steeply up into the darkness. Some of the steps had crumbled away completely, and large stones littered the floor around their feet.

'Well, that's why the wall was bricked up,' said Bert. 'This place is so rotten it's falling down.'

Ruby studied one of the stones. 'With just a little help, perhaps,' she said thoughtfully.

'What?' asked Bert.

'Come on, let's get this over and done with,' said Ruby. 'I ought to be getting home.'

'Right.'

Bert crept off down the passageway.

'Hang on a moment,' said Ruby suddenly, grabbing Bert and pulling him back. 'What's that? Down there.'

Bert shone his torch down a corridor that broke away at a right angle. The torchlight reflected off something metal.

'Do you think that's the laundry?' asked Ruby.

Bert didn't have enough time to answer; Ruby had already pushed him down the corridor. As they neared the door at the end, Bert shone his torch into the pitch black room.

'What can you see?' Ruby asked.

Rows of huge old top-loading washing machines

were assembled in a line, and wooden clothes 'dollies' hung down from the ceiling, suspended from pulleys.

'This is it,' said Bert.

Ruby peered over his shoulder. 'I can't see any tunnel opening,' she said.

'It'll be hidden,' said Bert. He shone the torch at the map. 'It's just a matter of finding it.'

Slowly they made their way round the room, scouring every inch of wall.

'It'll definitely be here somewhere,' said Bert.

'I really ought to be getting back,' said Ruby. 'Maybe the map's wrong.'

'No,' said Bert, studying one of the washing machines. 'The tunnel's definitely here somewhere. We just need to think of a way of opening it.'

He pushed against one of the old machines, tilting it back as he crouched down and peered at the stone floor underneath. With a loud crash, the machine fell back on to the floor. The noise reverberated through the corridors like rolling thunder.

'Right, that's it,' said Ruby, fed up now. 'This whole tunnel thing is plainly a load of nonsense. I think we should go. Now.'

'One more minute,' said Bert, on his hands and knees.

'Come *on!*' said Ruby, trying to find the door, and she leant on one of the ropes that held the drying rails up in the air.

Suddenly Bert felt a cold draught o[n] his neck, just like he had in the bathroom wh[en his] grandmother disappeared.

'Hang on! That's it. We're getting closer, Ruby. I can feel it.'

He turned round.

'Ruby?' he whispered.

Ruby had disappeared.

Bert sprang to his feet, wildly swinging his torch around the room.

'Ruby, this isn't very funny,' he called.

He stood and listened.

'I'll go back to the lift and leave you,' he said.

'I'm down here,' came Ruby's muffled voice.

Bert shone his torch down at the stone floor, only to find that the spot where Ruby had been standing had now sunk out of view. The paving stones had fallen to form a spiral staircase that dropped a few feet into the blackness.

'Ruby?' Bert called.

'Oh. My. Goodness. You're not going to *believe* what I've just found,' came her reply.

Bert pointed his torch into the stairwell and hurried down the steps. A dim glow grew stronger as he neared the bottom, and finally he burst out into a large tunnel lit by blazing torches. The ground was cobbled like an old street, and the walls were covered with paintings, similar to ones Bert had seen

churches. The tunnel
foot high, and the stone
into it, as if heavy carts had
. There was also writing, like
carved into the walls and ceiling. It
of the writing they'd seen in the vault.

gawped Bert. 'Now *this* is what I call a
hidden tunnel.'

'Come and take a look at this,' said Ruby, studying the wall opposite. '*Metuite. Belua resurget*. It's Latin.'

Bert ran his fingers over the letters. 'What does it mean?'

'Not sure. Something about "fear",' said Ruby. 'It's written over and over again. It must have taken ages to write. Years even. And look at all these numbers . . . Hang on a minute. That's a bit weird.'

'What?'

Ruby ran her fingers along the wall. 'These carved numbers,' she said. 'Some of them look quite recently cut.'

'Come on,' said Bert excitedly. 'Let's see where the tunnel goes.'

'You go,' said Ruby. 'I'm staying here. Just in case the staircase disappears again.'

'All right,' said Bert. 'Just a little way then.'

Bert grabbed Ruby's hand and pulled her down the tunnel. As they went, Bert noticed the mouths of huge pipes that appeared from out of the tunnel walls and dripped water on to the cobbles.

'This place is like a massive drain,' said Bert. 'I wonder where these pipes come from?'

'Can we go back yet?' asked Ruby.

'Just a little bit further.'

Suddenly Ruby grabbed Bert's shoulder. 'What's that noise?' she whispered.

'What noise?' asked Bert. 'I can't hear any noise?'

Slowly a quiet murmur grew into a louder roar, like the sound of a terrific waterfall.

'Oh my God!' hissed Ruby. 'Run!'

'No,' Bert said, and he clung on to Ruby's jumper. 'Wait.'

The rushing noise grew louder, until suddenly, from out of one of the enormous pipes surged a blast of water. And then a body swooped out of the pipe and flopped on to the cobbles like a rag doll. The water flow died, and the figure lay still on the wet stone floor in front of them.

'Who's that?' whispered Ruby, slowly backing down the tunnel. 'I don't like this, Robert. I think we should go.'

The figure stumbled to its feet, belching and gurgling. It was naked apart from a towel wrapped around its midriff and it wore a hat like a shower cap.

With a sudden cough, the figure heaved and spat something out. A moment later, a half-chewed toffee landed at Bert's feet. 'Oh my goodness,' he whispered. 'It's one of the Heaver sisters.'

'Who?'

'One of those old busybodies we saw earlier upstairs. But. What's she doing down here?'

'Urghhh,' groaned the old woman, stumbling on the slippery cobbles. 'Where am I?'

Bert and Ruby pressed themselves up against the tunnel walls so that they couldn't be seen.

'We ought to help her,' said Bert. 'But where's she come from?'

Suddenly a piercing scream echoed around them, followed by a snorting, gurgling sound, like a wild animal.

'Come on, Bert,' hissed Ruby.

And just as Bert was turning to go, a black figure crawled out of the darkness.

'Oh, dear Lord,' cried the old woman, as she backed away from the advancing creature. 'Help me. Somebody help me.'

Suddenly the creature pounced, grabbing the old lady and shaking her from side to side in its jaws.

Ruby tugged Bert's arm. 'RUN!' she yelled.

Trying not to catch his feet in the grooves on the cobbled floor, Bert sped back towards the staircase. Just as he was about to follow Ruby up the stairs, he shone his torch up the tunnel. The creature had finished with the old lady and was now staring down towards the staircase. Its eyes flashed red like a fox caught in car headlights. And then it started coming towards them. Bert froze momentarily.

'Oh my word, it's coming,' said Bert. 'It's coming after us!'

He pushed Ruby up the steps and out into the old laundry. His torch was now fading fast. Sprinting down the corridor, they came to the junction in front of the old staircase. The horrific snorting of the creature was getting closer behind them.

'Which way?' panted Ruby.

'I can't remember,' said Bert, trying to think.

'WHICH WAY?' yelled Ruby.

'Up here,' said Bert.

Holding Ruby's hand, Bert sped up the winding passage.

'There's the lift!'

As they both ran into the metal cage, heaving with exhaustion, Bert pulled the gate and lift door closed. The cry of the animal behind them had now turned into a bloodcurdling scream.

Bert pressed the lift button. Nothing happened.

'Come on, you stupid lift,' he shouted, pumping the button in and out.

The red eyes appeared in the gloom in front of them. Slowly the black figure stalked around the room, its heavy breathing sending shivers down Bert's spine.

'Come on, come on,' said Bert, getting more and more agitated. 'Please work.'

Suddenly Ruby threw her fist at the lift button.

'COME ON YOU STUPID HEAP OF JUNK!' she screamed.

The howling black figure leapt at the bars, just managing to grab on to Ruby's hair as the lift jolted into action.

'Ahhhhh!' yelled Ruby.

Bert spun round and as he was about to bring the heavy torch down on to the clutching limbs of the baying creature, he stopped. The animal let go, and the lift rose up towards the hotel. Ruby was left sprawled across the lift floor, clutching her scalp.

'It nearly had me,' she gasped, heaving for breath. 'That *thing* nearly had me.'

Bert collapsed on to the ground, his face white as a sheet.

'That *thing* was human,' he said.

Slowly the lift rose up out of the black depths, passing the gloomy lighting of the first basement, and up to the ground floor. And as the metal cage came to a rest, it 'pinged' cheerfully like a microwave, and the front gate automatically swung open.

Unaccustomed to the bright lights of the hotel hallway, Bert squinted out through the doors and could just make out a huge crowd of people gathering at the lift entrance. He and Ruby were both still lying on the cold metal floor, until suddenly he felt himself being lifted up into someone's arms.

'Robert? Son?' came his father's kind voice. 'Are you all right?'

Bert's sight was coming back to him. Hundreds of faces were peering in through the lift doors. Everybody was there: his grandfather, the priest, Ruby's dad, his mother.

'It got her, Dad,' Bert whispered weakly. 'There's something down there.'

'What? What was that?'

Bert felt himself being carried out into the hallway. The Coldstream Guards were playing over the tannoy.

'One of the Heaver sisters,' said Bert. 'She was eaten in front of our eyes, down in the lower basement.'

'You've been down to the lower basements?' shrieked his mother. 'How many times have we told you it's not safe down there?'

'Those ceilings could cave in at any moment,' came the voice of Ruby's dad.

'No, listen,' pleaded Bert. 'We saw one of the Heaver sisters down there. She's been taken, just like Granny was.'

As he looked over his father's shoulder, he was met by the piercing stare of the priest, his eyes black as coal.

'I think you must have had a nasty fall,' said his dad.

'Please believe me.'

'He's lying,' came the rumbling voice of the priest. 'Just like I told you.'

'But what about Miss Heaver?' asked Bert.

Bert's father swung his son around to face the staircase. There, descending the carpeted steps in their flowing evening gowns, were all three Heaver sisters, smiling demurely as they made their way to the dining room.

'Happy now?' asked his father.

Chapter Six

The bright morning sunshine glared in through Bert's open bedroom window and fell across his duvet. Outside, he could hear the curlews chattering as they danced above the tussock grass, while snippets of conversation floated in on the breeze as guests flip-flopped happily down to the beach.

Bert's mum checked her watch. 'OK, that'll do,' she said, and she whipped the thermometer out of her son's mouth. 'Hmm, just as I thought,' she said, 'a slight temperature. I think we'll keep you in bed today.'

'But Mum . . .'

'No buts. Doctor's orders.'

The chair scraped on the floor as she stood up and made her way across the room.

'This whole dreadful granny situation has plainly taken its toll. You need rest, Robert, and bed is the only place you're going to get it.'

'But I slept really well,' said Bert, having hardly caught a wink all night. 'How about I go and snooze out in the sun? On the cliff path . . .'

'No. It's bed and that's it,' she said, and she spun round and opened the door. 'I'll check on you at lunch-time.'

And with that she went, the key grating in the lock behind her.

Bert turned over and stared out of the window. He wondered how Ruby was being treated. He bet that *she* didn't get shut in her room.

Suddenly Tallulah's freckled face appeared through the window. 'Still dreaming of sca-a-ary monsters, Robert?' she said, cackling with laughter. 'Careful you don't get *eaten*.'

Bert leant over, closed the window and locked it for good measure.

'Such a shame you can't be joining us on the beach today,' she said, her voice muffled by the glass. 'Still, if you will go making up such stupid stories . . .'

Bert scowled at her and yanked the curtains closed. Lying back down, he pulled the duvet up over his shoulders and listened to his sister's laughter fading as she disappeared down towards the cliff path. Today was going to be so boring, he thought, and there were *so* many questions that were left unanswered.

As he lay there in the gloom, lost in his thoughts of what had taken place the day before, he gradually became aware of a quiet scratching noise nearby. It sounded like mice behind the skirting board. He rolled over and tried to ignore it.

'Robert?' came a voice.

Bert sat up, leant over and looked under his bed. The heap of old tennis raquets and his father's school tuck box hadn't moved for years. His mind was obviously playing tricks on him. Maybe he *did* need that rest.

'Robert!'

Bert jumped out of bed. He'd definitely heard it this time. He knelt down and pressed his ear to the floorboards.

'Not over there, you goon. Over here.'

'Grandpa?' whispered Bert.

The voice had come from the corner of the room, by the sink. He crawled across the floor and leant against the wall.

'Grandpa? Is that you?'

'I'm behind the mirror,' called the gaffer. He sounded agitated. 'I can't seem to get out.'

The mirror had been there for as long as Bert could remember. It hadn't been cleaned for years and rust had crept under the glass around the edges.

He tried to pull it off the wall, but it was stuck fast.

'There'll be a switch somewhere; probably hidden. It's just a matter of finding it.'

'Right,' said Bert, hunting around him. 'A switch. Erm . . .'

He picked up the toothbrush mug and chucked out the contents. He turned the taps on full, pulled out the plug, stuck his fingers down the overflow. Nothing seemed to work.

'Come on,' mumbled Bert under his breath. 'A hidden switch.'

He scoured the walls, the floor, even the horrible bit behind the sink where years of grime had collected.

'It must be there somewhere!' came his grandfather's voice again. 'It's probably right in front of your face.'

And then Bert spotted it, the old light hanging over the mirror with the gaudy glass lampshade. It hadn't worked for as long as he could remember. Bert pulled his chair over, climbed up on to it and pulled the tiny beaded cord that hung down beside the bulb. The light buzzed and flickered, but the mirror didn't move.

'Come on,' said Bert, repeatedly clicking it on and off again. 'This must be it.'

Suddenly the mirror shot up into the wall, and out from behind it toppled the gaffer, covered in brick dust. There was a thump as he hit his head on the porcelain sink and landed in a heap on the floor.

Bert looked down from the chair. 'Crikey,' he spluttered, laughing in disbelief. 'How did you get in there?'

The gaffer picked himself up from the floor, and rubbed his head furiously. His moth-eaten tweed jacket was torn and his trousers were filthy. 'Never mind all that,' he said gruffly. 'I need you to do something for me.'

Bert climbed down from his chair. 'But you've just fallen out of my bedroom wall!' he said, still a bit shellshocked. 'And you're covered in cobwebs.'

'Yes, yes, I know,' said his grandfather. He pulled the light cord again, and the mirror shot down back into place. 'I haven't used *that* tunnel since your father was born.'

'You *what*?' asked Bert.

'Look,' said his grandfather, kneeling down, 'unfortunately I don't have time to explain. It'll all become clear soon enough.'

'What'll become clear soon enough?'

'I need you to go shopping for me again,' said the gaffer. He pulled out a crumpled piece of paper from his jacket pocket and pressed it into Bert's hand. 'Mr Whicker's grocery shop.'

Bert looked into his grandfather's eyes. He looked tired, as if he hadn't slept for a week.

'Shopping? But I can't leave the room,' said

Bert. 'Mum's locked it. She'd kill me if she found out I'd gone.'

The gaffer pulled open the curtains, and unlatched the window, his mop of white hair swaying in the draught. 'Just get dressed,' he said.

Bert pulled his trousers from the top of his chest of drawers. 'This is about what Ruby and I saw yesterday, isn't it?' he said. The gaffer stared down at the floor, rubbing his face wearily. 'And it's about what we heard you and the priest discussing down in the vestry.' Bert tugged his trousers on over his pyjama bottoms, and slipped on his trainers. 'So why can't *you* go to the shops?' he asked. 'Your moped will go far quicker than my bicycle.'

'Robert, I'm needed here,' said the gaffer.

Bert stared at his grandfather for a moment. He grabbed his digital watch off his bedside table and climbed up on to the windowsill. 'I'll be back as soon as I can,' he said. The gaffer smiled weakly as Bert jumped out on to the gravel drive. 'Then you can tell me what's really going on.'

With the wind whistling through his hair, Bert sped along the hotel driveway and out on to the lane, weaving his bicycle around the puddles left by the rainstorm the night before. And as he rode down into the village and eventually burst out on to the cobbled high street, he found the heart of the village bustling with life. Bunting was being hung from lampposts, and the local brass band was practising by the harbour wall.

Hopping off his bike and resting it against the shop window, Bert darted into the grocery store before he was seen. The bell jingled as the door closed behind him.

'Who's that?' came the croaky voice of Mr Whicker.

Bert looked around the shop. It seemed empty. The familiar whistling and sucking of the printing press was coming from the back of the shop. Suddenly Mr Whicker's head appeared around the door behind the till.

'Go away,' he squawked, 'we're closed.'

Bert was a little startled. 'I've come to get some things for my grandfather,' he said, pulling the shopping list out of his pocket.

Mr Whicker's eyes narrowed. He shuffled out from behind the counter and snatched the note out of Bert's hand. 'Let me see,' he said.

Bert peered out of the window as Whicker read the list. 'What's going on outside?' he asked.

'It's the eclipse preparations,' mumbled Whicker. 'What does your grandfather want with insect repellent?'

Bert shrugged.

'Ten cans. Who does he think I am?'

The grocer picked up a wire basket from the stack by the door and hobbled off down one of the aisles, miaowing quietly to himself as he went.

Out of sight, Bert leant over the counter and peered through the door into the back room. It was a gloomy, hot place with no windows. A single chair stood in the centre, with cut-up bits of newspaper strewn on the floor. The old printing press was busy sucking in sheets of paper from a huge pile one end and regurgitating them out the other.

'Hey, wow! What are you printing?' asked Bert, scurrying around the counter and into the back room. An enormous ginger cat lying on top of the press spat and hissed as Bert picked up one of the wet printed sheets.

'Come to the eclipse,' he read out loud. 'Tomorrow, August 8th.'

Suddenly he got a clip round the ear.

'Mind your own business!' shouted Whicker, tearing the poster out of Bert's hands. 'And get out. This room's private.'

The cat seemed to smirk as it watched Bert leave.

'I thought you didn't keep cats, Mr Whicker,' said Bert as he fought with a piece of newspaper that had got glued to the sole of his shoe.

'I don't,' snapped Whicker.

On top of the counter, next to the till, was the shopping basket full of insect repellent and leg wax.

'Right,' croaked Whicker. 'It's all there. I presume you've got the cash?'

Bert plunged a hand into one of his pockets,

fishing around for the loose change his grandfather had given him. As he fought to dig out the money, he suddenly spied his mother crossing the street outside.

'Whoa! I'm done for!' shrieked Bert, diving behind the counter.

Whicker glared at Bert huddled down by his feet.

'You can't let her know I'm here, Mr Whicker,' whispered Bert frantically. 'Please?'

Whicker narrowed his eyes and thought for a moment.

Suddenly, the bell above the door jingled as his mum stepped inside.

'Ah, Mrs Twistleton, how delightful to see you,' said Whicker, snapping out of his trance.

'Mr Whicker, good morning.'

The door closed again behind her.

'I've come to see if the hotel posters are ready.'

Barely daring to breathe, Bert squatted underneath the till. He was only a couple of inches away from his mother's shoes, when two more cats sauntered around the base of the counter, straight past Bert, and headed into the back room. As soon as they spotted Bert, however, they stopped in their tracks, arched their backs and began to spit and hiss at him.

'What's that awful racket?' Bert heard his mother ask.

'Cats!' snapped Whicker, and he kicked the cats

away. 'Pssssssssht!' he hissed. 'Shoooo.' The cats howled as, caught by Whicker's boot, they flew into the back room.

'I didn't know you were a cat lover, Mr Whicker?' said Bert's mum.

'I'm not,' replied the shopkeeper curtly. 'I detest them. Vermin.' He grimaced, adjusted his woollen tie and forced a smile. 'Now, how's that delightful son of yours, Mrs Twistleton?'

'Robert?' said Bert's mother, a little taken back. 'How kind of you to ask.'

'I do like to take an interest in the community,' oozed Whicker odiously.

'Well, Robert's sadly ill at the moment. In bed. But I'll be sure to tell him you asked.'

Whicker trod on Bert's fingers. 'Please do. What a cheerful young man he is.' Bert wanted to cry out in pain. 'Now, the eclipse posters. Unfortunately they are not quite ready, Mrs Twistleton. Still drying.'

'Oh?'

Bert bit Whicker's leg.

'THISAFTERNOON!' yelped Whicker.

Mrs Twistleton jumped. Bert let go as Whicker shifted his foot.

'Yes, er . . . this afternoon. I'll deliver them up to the hotel before dinner.'

'Ah, right. That'll be fine,' said Mrs Twistleton, a little unsettled by the shopkeeper's behaviour. 'Now I ought to get moving. I have an appointment with the police officer, before I go home and prepare Robert's lunch. Good day, Mr Whicker.'

Bert listened to his mother walking across the shop floor. As the bell jingled and the door closed he slowly rose up off the floor, blowing on his fingers to try to cool them down. Whicker grinned at him.

'Thank you,' said Bert sharply.

'Now pay up, and get out.'

With his other hand, Bert pulled the money out of his trouser pocket. Whicker scraped the coins off the counter and threw them into the cash tray as Bert emptied the shopping basket into a couple of plastic bags.

'You don't look very ill to me,' said Whicker sourly, as he turned to go back to his printing.

Bert opened the shop door. A couple more cats darted into the shop.

'Oh, I'm not really,' he said. 'It's more of a punishment actually. Ruby H-B and I found some old tunnels under the hotel basement.'

Whicker stopped dead in his tracks. 'Tunnels?' he said, slowly turning around.

'Yeah,' said Bert. 'And there's something strange living down there. Although I think it was more of a *someone*.'

Whicker had started to cross the shop floor, his eyes twitching nervously. 'And you say you got down there through the hotel basements?' he asked.

Bert backed away nervously from the advancing

shopkeeper. 'Well sort of,' he said. 'There seem to be entrances everywhere. We came across some ancient maps in the old chapel . . .'

'Ah, Robert!' came an out-of-breath voice from behind him. 'Thank goodness I caught you.' Bert spun round. Ruby had her head stuck round the door behind him, wheezing as she tried to regain her breath. 'I saw you come in, but then I saw your mother too. We need to talk. Urgently,' she said.

'Ruby, you know Mr Whicker of course?' said Bert.

Whicker was bristling with excitement. He had begun to sweat and his eyes were almost popping out of his head. He'd even started miaowing incessantly. Ruby ignored him.

'Robert, it's about that carved writing we found,' she whispered.

Whicker grabbed Bert's shoulder. 'You found writing?' he squawked.

'Robert, I think we should talk about this elsewhere,' she whispered.

'No, no, no. Why don't you come through into the back?' said Whicker, his saliva beginning to froth and bubble at the corner of his mouth. 'It's more private back there. I might be able to help. I know a lot about tunnels.'

Ruby took Bert's other arm. 'Robert, I really think we should leave,' she said, eyeing up Whicker suspiciously.

Bert pulled himself free as Whicker grappled to

keep hold of him. 'Yes, I think you're right,' he said.

The shop bell jingled as the door closed, and Bert and Ruby pushed the bike across the street towards the harbour wall. Behind them, standing in the front window, the weaselish Mr Whicker watched them go, as half a dozen cats purred and rubbed themselves against his calves.

'I dug around in my father's bookshelves this morning,' said Ruby, 'and I came up with these.' She took a handful of books out of a knapsack, and placed them on her lap.

Bert shifted his bottom closer along the pontoon. '*The Language of Civilizations*,' he read out loud. 'Sounds thrilling.'

'Let's start with the numerals first,' said Ruby, ignoring the sarcasm. She opened up an old logbook on her lap.

'Numerals?' asked Bert.

'Those long lines of "V"s and "X"s carved into the tunnel walls. Roman numerals.'

'Oh *those*, right. Of course.'

'I was up all night trying to work out what they meant. I thought first of all that they must have been dates,' said Ruby. She took out a pen and wrote the numerals on a pad, separating the day, month and year.

Bert looked impressed. 'Me too,' he said, swishing his feet about in the water.

'Well, they are dates, but that's only part of it. The other numbers didn't seem to correspond to anything at all.'

'Just another load of meaningless maths then?' said Bert smiling.

'Not quite. If the "V"s and "I"s are translated into our ordinary numbers, like "5" and "1", then they fall into groups of eight digits.'

Ruby wrote them down. 'The same eight numbers repeating again and again,' she said.

Bert studied the long line of numbers Ruby had scrawled on to the pad. 'How did you remember all that?' he asked.

'I *am* the school swot, don't forget.'

Bert nodded. 'You certainly are,' he said.

'Well, the only other place I've seen numbers like that,' continued Ruby, 'is in my dad's fishing trawler logbooks.'

'I didn't know your dad was a fisherman *as well* as a service lift nut,' asked Bert.

'He's not. Not any more,' said Ruby. 'But, and this is the good bit, the answers are all there. In the logbook. They're *coordinates*.'

Bert felt like his brain had been tied into a knot. He stared at the logbook on Ruby's lap. 'I don't get it,' he said frowning.

'It's longitude and latitude, the way that distances around the earth are measured. The eight numbers are coordinates, or degrees north and south. They accurately pinpoint a place on the globe that can be found by anybody with a good enough chart.'

'Like a fishing chart?' asked Bert.

'Exactly.'

'Right,' said Bert, pleased he'd finally got there. 'So where's the pinpointed place then?'

'We can see it from here,' said Ruby, standing up. The pontoon rocked in the water as she pointed to the headland through the masts of the fishing trawlers. 'The Baloddan Hotel.'

'You're kidding,' said Bert, squinting into the distance. 'Well, that's brilliant. I don't need a load of numbers to tell me where the hotel is. I live there.'

Ruby grabbed his shirt-sleeve and pulled him back down again. 'Yes, but when all the dates and coordinates are brought together,' she said, circling the numbers in the book, 'then we have the exact place and time for an event that's been *foreseen* to take place. An event that may have been foreseen hundreds of years ago.'

'Oh, right, yes, of course,' he said, embarrassed. 'So something's due to happen in the hotel?'

'Apparently,' said Ruby.

'So what is it?'

Ruby paddled her feet in the water.

'Well, that's the tricky bit,' she said. 'I don't know. I couldn't work it out. I *think* it refers to some sort of resurrection, "*Resurget*" means "will rise again". I think.'

Bert looked a little concerned. 'Resurrection? Doesn't sound very good, does it?' he said.

'I might be wrong of course. The writing in the tunnel's not quite the same as the Latin in any of these books. I think it's religious. The word "*deus*" means "god" according to this dictionary.'

Bert looked blank.

'Look, what is clear,' said Ruby, 'is that we need to do more research. In the library.'

'I'm not sure I've got the time right now,' said Bert, looking at his watch. 'I've got to be back by lunch.'

Ruby turned and stared at Bert.

'I'm not sure any of us have the time, Robert,' she said sternly. 'Look at the date this *resurrection* happens.' She pointed at the numbers she'd translated in her notebook.

'Tuesday August eighth?' said Bert. 'But that's tomorrow.'

'The solar eclipse,' said Ruby.

Chapter Seven

From the narrow, cobbled street outside, the Baloddan Library looked like many of the buildings in the village. It was constructed from local stone with gabled lead windows, and an upper story that hung out over the lane below. Over the centuries, the structure had shifted and now the whole building leant precariously down towards the harbour.

'This place looks like it's about to fall down,' said Bert, leaning his bike against the wall.

'Come *on*,' said Ruby impatiently. 'It'll be lunch-time soon. We haven't got all day.'

The heavy front door opened up into an enormous hall, with rows of bookshelves running from end to end. Around the edge of the room were small tables with reading lamps and plaques on the walls that read SILENCE.

'Can I help you, my dears?' quivered an elderly lady sitting behind the librarian's desk in front of them.

'We're looking for the local history section,' whispered Ruby.

'Hmmm,' wondered the old lady, sucking on her gums as she thought for a moment. Bert wondered how old she was; her face had pockmarks from too much sun, and the skin on the back of her hands looked waxy and translucent with age.

'Well . . .' she pondered. 'I think it may be towards the back. Or maybe it's closer to the front. No, no, I was right the first time . . .'

Bert winked at Ruby. 'Not to worry,' he said to the old lady. 'We'll find it.'

The librarian smiled sweetly and Bert and Ruby scoured the rows of bookshelves for anything that looked relevant. There were titles on cooking, gardening, crochet, geriatric health problems, in fact everything other than what they were looking for. After ten minutes, Bert sat down on a footstool for a rest, when suddenly he spotted a door in the far corner of the room. The words 'Restricted Viewing' were written in white across the frosted glass pane.

Bert looked about. Ruby had disappeared behind another bookshelf. Quietly, Bert crept over to the door, twisted the handle and, checking no one was watching, disappeared inside. As he closed the door behind him, he fumbled for the light switch. With a zap, the neon strip flickered to life, revealing that the room obviously doubled as the librarian's office. A large desk sat in the middle, with a teapot and packet of digestive biscuits neatly arranged to one side. A coat and handbag hung on a hatstand behind the door. The walls were lined with books. Bert wandered around the room reading the cracked book spines for anything that might seem relevant. He found nothing. Disappointed, he made to leave.

Just as he was about to flick the light off, however, he spotted a tiny sepia photograph in a frame sitting on one of the shelves. There was something familiar about the man and two children in the picture. Proudly sticking their chests out, they stood in front of an army of bricklayers wearing cloth caps and smoking pipes. Bert reached up to take the photo down. But when, with a slight tug, the picture finally came away from the shelf, there was a loud grating sound and the whole wall in front of him sprung open.

He could hardly believe his eyes as behind the shelf appeared a hidden cupboard, stacked with old photographs and piles of books. There were alphabetically labelled box files arranged in rows, and the walls were plastered with newspaper cuttings. In the centre, on a small shelf, were dozens of candles, some still burning, as though the cupboard was a sort of shrine.

'Oh my goodness,' mumbled Bert to himself, peering closer at the newspaper cuttings around him. Each article was about a mysterious disappearance, just like the photos he'd found in the hidden room next to the gaffer's bedroom. The cuttings themselves looked old and discoloured. Bert pulled down one of the books. *Baloddan Since the Eleventh Century* read the title.

'Bingo,' said Bert. He hurried over to the door and stuck his head out into the library. 'Ruby,' he whispered loudly.

Ruby peered out from behind a bookshelf. Looking about, she hurried over to him.

'What on earth are you doing?' she hissed. 'You need permission to go in there.'

'You'll never guess what I've found.'

'I don't care,' said Ruby. 'We might get caught, and then thrown out, and then we won't find a *thing*, and it'll all be your . . .'

Bert opened the door to reveal the candlelit wardrobe.

'Fault,' said Ruby, rather gobsmacked. 'Goodness.'

'I think it's a shrine or something,' said Bert. 'And it's stuffed with books on the village.'

Ruby walked over and peered in. 'But . . . this cupboard was hidden?'

'Yeah, I found it by mistake. I tried to pull down

this old photograph.' Bert studied the picture a bit more carefully. 'It seems to be a shot of the hotel. And I think that's my grandfather when he was a kid,' he mumbled. 'And that must be my great-grandfather. Not sure who the *girl* is though.'

Ruby picked out a couple of books. 'But why would anyone want to hide *this* lot? And burn candles, that's *really* weird.'

She sat down and put the books down on the desk. Licking her fingers she turned the pages and started to read, while Bert took down a few of the articles from the cupboard walls.

'Miss Felicity Redmond,' he mumbled to himself, reading the first newspaper strip. 'Sounds familiar.'

'How peculiar,' said Ruby, now getting stuck into the books. 'Robert, do you know of any abbeys round here?'

Bert thought hard. 'Nope,' he said.

'Funny. Neither do I, but I think this book's a diary. Of a monk or someone.'

'Felicity Redmond again!' said Bert, waving another article in the air. 'Died in 1943. Golly, I knew these articles were old.'

'Whoever wrote this seems to name Baloddan quite a lot,' said Ruby, her head still buried in the book.

'And again!' said Bert. 'All of these newspaper cuttings are about this Redmond woman.'

'Ah, here we are. There's a drawing here,' mumbled Ruby, opening up a second, heavier book.

'Miss Felicity Elspeth Redmond, 85, of Baloddan, North Cornwall,' continued Bert, reading a third article out loud. 'Died yesterday in a freak case of Spontaneous Human Combustion. Although no body has been recovered, police are still at the scene in the lower floors at the local . . .'

'Robert, didn't you mention the other day that the hotel had been involved in a fire?'

'That was ages ago,' said Bert. 'Hundreds of years ago, I think.'

'But what was on the site before the hotel? What was burnt down?'

'I don't know. Listen to this . . .'

'Robert, I think I've just found out.'

'Yes, yes, but . . .'

'It was a monastery. A twelfth-century mediaeval monastery.'

'Will you listen to me for one moment? Please?' shouted Bert, slamming a cutting down on to the table. He pointed frantically at the black and white photo. 'These articles. They're all written about—'

'Me,' came a low, coarse voice.

Ruby spun round. The librarian was standing in the doorway. Her stooped back had now completely vanished, and her breathing sounded heavy and rasping.

'You think you're so clever, don't you, Robert Twistleton?' she hissed, stepping further into the room. 'Snooping around, messing in other people's business.'

'Felicity Redmond,' said Ruby, reading out her name badge.

'Her photo was in that hidden room with your aunt's,' Bert whispered. 'That's where I'd seen her name before.'

'You're going to regret coming in here. You haven't a clue what you've got yourself involved in.'

'But you died in . . . 1943,' quivered Ruby. 'Aged 85. That's impossible. That makes you . . .'

'Far too old to be alive,' said the woman, stepping closer. Her eyes had started to flash red and, as she bowed down to Ruby's height, she cackled like a hyena. 'But Felicity Redmond's dead, remember? Hahaha.'

'Look at her hands!' screamed Bert.

The skin on the old lady's hands was bubbling, and steam had started to rise off her back.

'Say goodbye to your friend, Robert,' she hissed and she drew back, ready to pounce on Ruby.

Suddenly Bert brought his grandfather's heavy shopping bags down on the librarian with all the force he could muster.

'Run!' he yelled, as the librarian collapsed on the desk.

Ruby grabbed the book and they sprinted out of the room.

'Come back here!' howled the gargoyle-like

librarian, as she fought to get to her feet, but Bert and Ruby were already out through the doors.

Outside, Bert grabbed his bike, swung the plastic bags through the handlebars, and ran with it down the street.

'What do we do now?' asked Ruby, checking that the librarian wasn't following.

'We get home,' said Bert, gasping for breath. 'I need to speak to the gaffer. There's something he's not telling us.'

'I'll try to find out more about the monastery,' said Ruby, panting. 'I want to know what's happened to my aunt.'

Bert stopped and grabbed Ruby's hand. 'Something bad's going on. I'm not sure how it's all connected, but if you're right about the eclipse, we've only got twenty-four hours to work this all out.' He jumped on to his bike. 'Now run. Before Felicity Redmond catches us.'

'Call me!' Ruby shouted as she ran down the high street, but Bert had disappeared round the corner, towards the cliff path.

Speeding along the top of the cliffs, with the waves crashing against the rocks below, Bert focused on the hotel in the distance. With his heart pounding and thoughts racing through his head, it wasn't until he finally approached the hotel that he noticed the police car pulling up in the driveway. Bert slammed on the brakes and dropped to the ground. As he lay hidden in the tussock grass, he watched the local constable and his mother get out of the car. Together they strode across the gravel towards the front doors of the hotel, their conversation floating on the breeze. Bert crawled closer.

'Yes, Mr Grimes,' his mother said, the stones crunching under her feet. 'Please consider yourself our guest for the day. If you have any questions for me or my family, don't hesitate to ask.'

'Thank you, Mrs Twistleton,' said the police officer, as he took off his helmet and followed her in through the doors. 'My enquiries shouldn't take too long.'

Bert looked at his watch; it was ten to one. His mother was late home. She probably hadn't started to make lunch yet. Bert had a little time to get back to his room before she checked on him, and then he could find the gaffer.

Keeping low, he picked up his bike and pushed it over to the kitchen window. He watched as his mother took off her coat, filled the kettle and plugged it into the mains. As she turned her back again, he ducked down, crawled under the window and shot round the side of the building, checking each window as he passed it. Just as he was trying to prise the bathroom window off its latch, he suddenly felt a presence behind him.

'Robert!'

Bert peered over his shoulder. It was the three fat Heaver sisters, each wearing a garish floral swimsuit and with a tight rubber swimming cap stretched over her head.

'What on earth are you doing?' wheezed the first sister.

'Breaking and entering?' asked the second.

The third mumbled incoherently as she chewed on a toffee.

Bert eyeballed them all carefully. Which one's the impostor? he wondered. Which sister had he seen down below the basements? 'I was just, um, checking for, er . . . wood rot. In the window frames. A maintenance job for my father,' he said, forcing a smile.

'Right,' said the first sister haughtily. 'Well, don't let us stop you. We have lunch waiting for us.' Like three sumo wrestlers, they wobbled their way towards the back entrance, and disappeared inside, a whiff of burnt skin catching at the back of Bert's throat as they went.

As soon as they were out of sight, Bert jumped back down on to the grass, and picked up his grandfather's shopping bags. There was only one truly safe way into the house without being noticed, he thought, and that was the coal chute by the kitchen door. Darting back round the building, Bert opened the wooden hatch outside the hotel kitchens.

He dropped the plastic bags down into the darkness and then climbed down himself. Slowly he closed the hatch doors over his head and slid down the chute towards the basement. With a heavy thud, he landed in the gloom, straight on top of the gaffer's shopping.

'Hello? What do we have here?'

Suddenly a blinding light was shone straight in Bert's face.

'Robert Twistleton? I thought you were supposed to be ill?'

Bert reeled back from the bright torch beam. 'Who is it?' he asked, cowering from the light.

Suddenly an arm grabbed him and helped him up. With the torchlight out of his eyes, Bert could just make out the police officer.

'What are *you* doing down here?' asked Bert, trying not to sound impertinent.

'I could ask the same of you. Your mother told me you were in bed and not to be disturbed.'

Bert pulled his arm free. 'I had to go shopping for my grandfather,' he said.

'Ah yes, your elusive grandfather,' said Grimes. 'Doesn't seem to want to talk to the police either.'

Bert's eyes had become more accustomed to the dim lighting now. He carefully studied the officer's face in the gloom, the black hairs protruding from both nostrils.

'So what *are* you doing down here in the

basements?' he asked cautiously. 'It's easy to get lost down here.'

The police officer swung his torch beam around the pokey coal hole.

'Well, to tell you the truth, Mr Twistleton, I'm already rather lost,' he said. He looked back at Bert and knelt down. 'How about you help me find the boiler room, and I agree not to tell your mother you've been down to the village?' he said. 'Deal?' The police officer held out his hand for Bert to shake.

Bert thought for a moment. 'This *is* to do with the enquiry into my grandmother's disappearance?' he asked. 'Isn't it?'

The officer nodded.

'OK. I'll help you find the boiler room, if you help me get into my room without being seen *and* you don't say a word to my mother.'

'All right,' said the policeman.

'Deal then,' said Bert, and he shook the officer's hand enthusiastically.

Picking up the shopping, Bert led the police officer down through the basement passages. As they went, Bert flicked various light switches to light up the gloom. Finally they approached a small, blue, painted door with the words 'Boiler room – Keep out' scratched into the wood. Bert pushed it open.

'Hmm,' said the police officer. He ducked down

through the door, straightened up again the other side and walloped his head on one of the lead pipes. 'Ow!' he growled.

'About my grandmother's disappearance . . .' said Bert thoughtfully.

'Your grandmother hasn't disappeared, Robert. She's *dead*,' said the officer, rubbing his head. 'We just can't seem to find her body. And if you were to ask my opinion, we *won't* find it either.'

'But you said she was sucked down the loo?' said Bert.

'She was. And if she were coming back alive, like everybody else seems to round here, we'd have found her by now. But not your grandmother; she's gone for good. And it's my job to find out what's happened.'

Bert clicked on the light. With a 'plink', the bulb flickered and then went out again. He pulled the cord again. Nothing.

'Great,' said the officer. Flashing his torch around in the darkness, he found a room full of pipes intertwined with each other as they wound their way around the walls. Against the far end stood a massive boiler tank with pressure gauges and huge iron taps. The policeman walked up to it and patted it. 'Ah, this is the baby I was looking for.'

He examined the tank from every angle, eventually getting down on his hands and knees and peering underneath it. He even stuck his head down a dark, open manhole in the floor. 'Pwoarrrrrr!' he groaned, clutching his nose.

'Look, I know you're busy, officer, but I just need to ask one more question,' said Bert, his mind still on his grandmother. 'If you're convinced my granny has passed away, and you don't expect to find her body, then ... what exactly are you doing down here?'

The policeman looked up at Bert and narrowed his eyes. 'That's what I wanted to talk to *you* about, actually,' he squawked. He pulled a piece of paper from inside his jacket and shone the torch beam at it. 'This got pushed under the station door some time last night.'

He flashed the page in front of Bert's face. The writing had been cut out from pieces of newspaper, each word stuck clumsily to the note.

Bert read the sentence out loud. ' "Don't give up on the Twistleton case. Try the boiler room under the hotel." ' He frowned. 'Golly,' he said. 'Who wrote that?'

The policeman shrugged. 'That's the next thing I've got to find out.'

Suddenly Bert noticed a strange shape appear in the darkness, around the rim of the manhole behind the officer.

'I might not be from around these parts, but I know when there's something weird going on. And there's something *very* weird about this village.'

It was a hand – a bony, warty hand.

The officer bent down to Bert's height, and stared deep into his eyes. 'No one seems to die here in Baloddan,' he whispered.

Bert gulped.

'People disappear all right. A bit too regularly if you ask me. But soon enough most of them come back. Alive.'

Bert shivered and started to back away from the police officer, as out from the manhole rose a black figure. He couldn't make out the face or ragged clothing, but the silhouette had all the limbs of a human being, and its eyes flashed red as it turned and glared at Bert.

'That's why Baloddan's full of so many pensioners. Everybody's in on it, but no one mentions it. They're afraid.' The policeman straightened up again. 'Now, I might be the laughing stock of the other officers in the station,' he continued, 'but I reckon I'm pretty close to finding out what's *really* been going on around here.'

Bert had frozen to the spot, the colour draining from his face.

'So close, in fact, that someone's been trying to shut me up. Someone's trying to put me off the scent by sending me on wild goose chases. But you wait and see, I'll get to the bottom of this. I'll find out the truth . . .'

Grimes stopped.

'Are you all right there, son?' he asked, shining the torch straight in Bert's face. 'You look a bit peaky.'

Suddenly the black creature behind him turned and stretched open its gaping jaws, its whole head doubling in size. As Bert lifted his arm and pointed over the officer's shoulder, Grimes slowly began to turn to see what was behind him.

'What the—?'

With the speed of a bullwhip, the black figure flicked out its insect-like tongue, wrapped it around the police officer and dragged him off his feet. Grimes howled as the horrific monster swallowed him and the torch whole.

Bert spun round and tried to run, but the door handle came away in his hand. Slowly turning back, he realized he was helpless in the total darkness. He heard the creature belch and crawl closer, its wet feet squelching on the boiler room floor.

'No, no, please. Not me,' Bert pleaded as he pressed himself against the wall, shaking in terror.

He could smell the acrid stench of the creature's breath. He could feel the piercing glare of its red eyes, as it inhaled his scent through its nostrils. And as he squeezed his eyes tight shut and thought that he too was about to be eaten, he felt the creature lean out and stroke his face gently. Bert's blood ran cold, as it ran its leathery fingers across his cheek so delicately that he could hardly feel it at all.

Bert didn't even flinch for what seemed like a lifetime. Finally, as he shivered in the cold, he opened an eyelid to find the creature's red eyes had vanished.

Chapter Eight

'Where have you been, you disobedient child?' squawked Mrs Twistleton.

Bert shuffled his feet awkwardly on the stone slabs as his mum waited for an answer.

'Well?'

'I was down in the boiler room . . .' mumbled Bert.

His mum took his slime-covered jumper in both hands and shook Bert violently. 'I know that! Your father told me *that*!' she shrieked. A plastic roller fell out of her hair and bounced on the hall floor by Bert's feet. 'You were *supposed* to be ill in bed! That's where I left you. Can't you do anything you're asked to?'

Bert looked at his dad for some help. His dad shrugged.

'But it wasn't my fault,' said Bert. 'Grandpa . . .'

'Don't you *dare* bring your grandfather into this. He's got enough problems of his own for you to start dragging him in.'

Bert's eyes started to well up. His father butted in.

'Robert was unconscious when I found him, dear. Mumbling something about that police officer. I think he must have banged his head as one of the pipes burst.'

His mother stood up straight, holding on to the bath towel wrapped around her body. 'You don't say, Leonard,' she said sarcastically.

'I beg your pardon, dear?'

Spotting an opportune moment, Bert turned and headed towards his bedroom door. His head throbbed and he felt like going to bed.

'Robert, go and get washed and changed. We've got the eclipse meeting tonight.'

'Darling,' interrupted Mr Twistleton, 'don't you think . . .'

'Leonard, if our son is well enough to disappear down into the basement when he's supposed to be feeling ill, then he's well enough to help out next door.'

'Right, dear.'

Bert opened his bedroom door and disappeared inside. The curtains were closed, and a tray of cold lunch was sitting on his duvet.

'You know, Leonard,' Bert heard his mum say out in the hall, 'that boy can sometimes really test my patience.'

'Right, dear,' said Bert's father.

'And I know exactly where he gets it from.'

Bert shuddered as a door slammed.

'Yes, dear.'

As Bert stared at his filthy face in the bedroom mirror, he considered everything that had happened to him in the past few days. He'd been present when two people had got eaten, heard evidence of a third, and been stroked by the very creature who'd eaten all three. His grandfather had started appearing out of walls, he'd somehow become friends with the school swot and no one, not even his parents, believed a single word he said. It seemed to Bert that, as he picked the stinking green muck out of his ears, he was standing on the edge of a precipice. He couldn't go back as he'd found out too much, and ahead of him things promised to get much, much worse.

He ran the taps and cleaned his face with a flannel before he dug out a clean pair of trousers and shirt from his wardrobe. Soon he looked unrecognizable from the stinking creature that had walked through the door minutes earlier. And with his hair combed into a side parting, he moved the tray of food and lay on his bed, waiting for his father to call him.

The minutes flicked past as the curtains

sporadically glowed as car after car pulled up in the driveway outside. Eventually, having picked at the cold lasagne in front of him, he started to nod off, until quite suddenly he heard a scratching noise from the other side of the room. Squinting into the gloom, he could just make out an object being pushed underneath the door.

'Hello?' he called out as he got to his feet. 'Is somebody there?'

A small blank envelope was lying on the floorboards. He picked it up, slid his finger under the flap and tore the letter open. It stank of insect repellent, and his grandfather's messy writing spewed across the page.

> 'Robert. I need your help urgently. We must talk. Alone. Attached is a map. Get here as soon as you can.'

Suddenly the door burst open, walloping Bert on exactly the same spot as the bump on his forehead, knocking him back on to the floor. His dad walked in.

'Pom pom pom tiddly . . . Ooh, Robert, what are you doing on the floor?'

Bert heaved himself up on to his feet again.

'Got a letter, have we?' asked his dad.

Still feeling a little unsteady, Bert hid the note behind his back.

His father sniffed the air and smiled. 'Hmmm, perfume. Is it from Mr H-B's daughter?' he asked. 'Heard you've been seeing a bit of her recently.'

Bert blushed. 'Who told you that?' he asked, squashing the note into his pocket.

'Oh, Mrs Thingummy Redmond from the village library. She's come up for the meeting next door. First time we've seen her for years.'

Bert turned white as a sheet. 'Mrs Felicity Redmond?'

'Something like that. Never mind. Come on, wouldn't be diplomatic to keep your mother waiting this evening,' and Mr Twistleton pushed his son out into the apartment hall.

Bert fumbled for an excuse to stay behind as his father edged him closer and closer to the hotel lobby. His heart was pounding, almost in time with the thumping military band music blaring out over the tannoy system the other side of the apartment door.

'Where would we be without the Coldstream Guards, eh, Robert?' chuckled his father merrily.

Thwatthwat went the door on its sprung hinges, as they exited into the hotel.

The huge dining room on the other side of the foyer had been used as a ballroom in Victorian times. Vast chandeliers still hung from the ceiling, and large round tables lined what was once the dance floor.

'Excuse me,' said Bert as he and his father

squeezed past the crowd milling by the door. The room swarmed with waiters buzzing round the hundreds of guests, clearing the main course and delivering trays of steaming pudding. Suddenly Bert's mum appeared at the swing doors into the kitchen.

'Ah finally,' she said, looking at her watch. 'Robert, why don't you go and stand up at the front with your sister, while your father and I talk for a moment.'

His father looked terrified as his wife yanked him in through the doors. Bert continued to work his way down the edge of the room, stepping over the feet of the staff members and locals sitting against the wall.

'Evening, Robert,' said Mr Dawbany, dressed from head to foot in his spandex Captain Fabulous outfit. Elvis the Wonder Dog was cowering by his feet, baring his teeth at the chirpy Mr Whicker, who was sitting a couple of chairs down.

Suddenly a sleek, black leather boot appeared, blocking Bert's path. Father Hooper, dressed from head to foot in his customary black, leant down to him and sneered. 'Evening, Robert,' he growled, his eyes as dark as coal.

Bert tried to smile.

The priest whispered in his ear, 'I know you're up to something, Twistleton. When I find out what, you'll wish you'd never been born.'

Bert pushed his way past, almost tipping the fat

lady opposite off her chair, and scurried down to the front of the room.

His sister Tallulah scowled as he fell into place beside the podium. 'You're late,' she spat.

Bert scanned the crowd in front of him. He recognized most of the faces at the tables: Mr Tuttle, the Heaver sisters, and the gargoyle-like features of Felicity Redmond, who was squatting in a seat at the front. Her pencil-thin lips curled into a toothless smile as she winked at him. Bert shivered.

Suddenly the lights went down, the marching music jerked to a stop, and Bert's mother glided into the room from the kitchen. The crowd broke into applause as she made herself comfortable at the podium.

'Ladies and Gentlemen, friends and guests,' she called, projecting her voice to the back of the room. 'As you all know by now the first solar eclipse over Cornwall for almost eight hundred years will be taking place tomorrow.'

As his mum droned on about the list of events and charity tombolas that were due to take place over the next couple of days, Bert pulled his grandfather's note from his back pocket. The map seemed to be a plan of another tunnel complex, and judging by a large 'X' beside the word 'dumbwaiter', the entrance was somewhere in the kitchen. But what on earth was a dumbwaiter? Bert thought it was time to find out. He crossed his legs and leant over to his sister.

'Just off to the loo,' he whispered. 'Back in a second.'

Tallulah looked at him in total horror. 'You can't do that now!' she hissed, her pigtails flapping wildly. 'You'll ruin Mum's big speech.'

'Sorry, can't hold it in.'

Bert squeezed past her. With a chorus of tutting and disapproving jowl wobbles coming from the lined-up members of staff, he fought his way to the waiters' door. And as he pushed his way through into the kitchen, over two hundred and fifty pairs of eyes watched him disappear.

The kitchen was a hive of noisy activity as an army of chefs, staff and waiters charged around carrying trays of scalding hot food. With pots and pans chattering and bubbling, and steam billowing from churning dishwashers, Bert weaved his way through the maze of legs and stainless steel ovens, desperate not to be spotted and thrown back out into the dining room.

'Who the hell let these cats in here?' yelled the familiar Spanish tones of the head cook.

A moggy shot past as Bert squashed himself into a tiny space between a freezer and a plate cupboard.

'Can someone *please* shut that flaming door?'

Slam.

'Ham, egg and chips ready for room 342.'

A howling scream as another cat got booted out of the way.

'Ham, egg and chips ready for room 342.'

Which of the waiters was dumb?

'Ham, egg and chips for room . . .'

'Got it.'

A pair of legs, in chequered trousers and white clogs, hurried up to Bert, close enough for him to touch. Bert froze whilst plates clattered above his head. Another cat screamed as it got flung out of the window, while the owner of the chequerboard trousers reversed, crossed the room and shoved the tray into a small, square hole in the wall. He then leant right in with the food tray.

'Ham, egg and chips, room 342!' he shouted. He gave a sharp tug on a rope that ran down the inside of the cupboard and slid the door closed. Bert was bewildered. He was even more astonished when a few seconds later, the same man reopened the doors and the food tray was gone.

Scratching his head, he took another look at the map in his pocket. Beside the 'X', his grandfather had written the words 'Close the doors and tug the rope three times'. Bert fixed his eyes on the food lift opposite him. Bingo, he thought. The dumbwaiter.

Taking a deep breath, Bert burst out of his hiding place, shot across the steaming kitchen and leapt straight into the hole in the wall.

'What the hell?'

'What's that kid doing in here?'

'Stop that brat!'

He slid the doors closed, and quickly tugged on the rope three times in the darkness.

Nothing happened.

'Get that flaming kid out of the food lift!' screamed a booming voice from the kitchen. Bert leant on the door handle with all his weight, desperate not to be caught. Suddenly, the platform he was sitting on jolted and started to drop. Letting go of the handle, Bert and the food lift broke into free fall as the brick wall and rope whistled past him. Further and further down the lift fell, until suddenly there was heavy thud, the lift halted abruptly and Bert whacked his already bruised head on the ceiling.

'Ow!' he yelled as he toppled out of the lift into the darkness.

His scream echoed around him in the pitch black. He sat up and rubbed his head.

'Hello?' he asked tentatively. 'Grandpa?'

His words died away into the abyss.

Bert was already wishing he'd paid more attention to the map in his pocket. Now he couldn't read a thing. He got to his feet and fumbled around. A cool draught of wind blew against his face as the lift hurtled back up to the kitchen.

'Grandpa?' he called. 'It's Robert.'

With each step forward, away from the lift, he felt a crunching, popping sensation under his shoes, as if he was walking on eggshells. Leaning down, he felt the ground, longing for a clue as to where he might be. To his surprise the floor seemed to be alive. A moving, squirming, seething mass of . . . He stood bolt upright as he felt something crawl up his leg. The ground beneath him was alive with insects.

Leaping up and down, Bert violently shook his trousers, but before he could scream, he felt another draught of wind against his face, and a clattering sound erupted from above him. If he wasn't mistaken the food lift was hurtling back down. He jumped as the platform crashed to the ground in the darkness.

Bert wondered what to do next.

'Hello?' he asked, starting to feel a little scared. 'Is that you, Grandpa?'

Slowly a low, coarse chuckle emanated out of the blackness.

'Hello?' came a reply. 'Is that you, Grandpa?'

Bert shook his head. He thought he was going mad. It sounded like his own voice.

'Who is it?' he asked, slowly backing away.

Silence.

'Please tell me who it is.'

Again the quiet laughter.

'Who is it?' came the voice. *His* voice. 'Please tell me who it is.'

Bert turned and started to walk a bit quicker through the pitch darkness. He was starting to sweat.

'If this is a joke, it isn't very funny,' he said.

'On the contrary,' came the voice. It sounded evil, almost as cold as the air around him. '*I'm* enjoying this immensely.'

Bert had broken into a jog. The insects crunched under his feet, cobwebs caught against his face, as the sound of heavy footsteps followed him in the darkness.

'Run, Robert, run. Your grandfather can't help you this time,' came the voice again, laughing manically. 'You're on my territory now.'

Bert cried out for help as he sprinted through the void. Suddenly he felt a strong hand grip his shoulder, pulling him off his balance. With a flash of light, Bert flew through the air and landed with a crunch on the ground. Temporarily winded by the fall, he gasped for air as he opened his eyes to find himself lying in a narrow stone corridor. Standing over him was his grandfather, who slammed a heavy door closed in front of him. With the ear-splitting grating of metal, the gaffer hurriedly drew several iron bolts across the door, and then stood back and waited.

'Grandpa?' said Bert, confused.

The gaffer put his hand on Bert's head. 'Don't worry,' he said. 'You're safe now.'

Suddenly the hinges and bolts of the door shook as whoever had been chasing Bert hammered against the wood like a crazed animal.

'You can't run for ever, you Twistletons,' came the

screaming voice from the other side of the door. 'I'll get you soon enough.'

The gaffer held on to the wall as a bloodcurdling roar shook the corridor around them, and then a deafening boom, as whoever or whatever it was threw its full and considerable weight at the door. The frame started to splinter. The gaffer picked up a canvas bag and helped Bert to his feet.

'Come on, Robert. I don't think we should hang around.'

Together they darted through weaving tunnels lit by flaming torches, as behind them they heard the repeated crashes of the door being battered.

'Those bolts are strong, but they won't last for ever,' said the gaffer. 'We need to make as much ground as we can before they give way.'

Bert was gasping for breath. 'I need to stop,' he said. 'Just for a moment.'

Watching out behind them, the gaffer let go of Bert, who immediately fell to the floor.

'What *was* that?' he panted. 'It had my voice. It sounded just like me. What's going on, Grandpa?'

'I'm not sure,' said the gaffer, looking back down the corridor, 'but whatever or whoever it was, it's clever all right. It seems to be able to mimic anyone and anything.'

'Mimic?' said Bert.

'It can take on the features of whoever it pleases.' The gaffer hesitated. 'They all can.'

'There's more than one?'

Boom! The door behind them sounded like it was getting weaker, as with every crash came an even greater splitting of wood.

'Come on,' said the gaffer. 'We must keep going.'

They started to run again. Soon they reached another door, this time built of reinforced steel. Keeping an eye on the corridor behind them, the gaffer took out a key from under his jumper. He pushed it into the lock, turned it and opened the door. Behind them they heard the previous door split and finally give way.

'Get in,' said the gaffer. 'These things can move like the wind.'

Bert darted through the door, quickly followed by his grandfather, who heaved it closed behind him. He locked it with the key and brought a heavy metal bar down across it with a crash.

'There, that should keep it off for a bit.'

Bert looked about him. They had entered a room about the size of a football pitch, with a high vaulted ceiling. Dozens of tables and workbenches spread out across the brick floor in front of him, each surface covered with an array of brightly coloured vacuum cleaners, various engine parts, and the odd pot of leg wax. The gaffer dashed across the room with his empty canvas bag.

'This is your work room?' said Bert, gazing at the machinery. 'Is this where you invent everything?' His grandfather remained silent as he stood against the far wall, keying numbers into a security pad on a huge metal safe. 'What about the letter you slipped under my door then? You needed to talk urgently.'

The safe door hissed as it opened, and the gaffer lifted something heavy out and deposited it in the bag. Bert couldn't see what it was, but its metal surface glinted in the light. The gaffer zipped the bag up and heaved it back over to Bert.

'Robert, I know what you and Ruby have been up to.'

'You do?'

'I know you saw the creature feeding under the old laundry. I know about the boiler room. But whatever's behind us now is small fry. What you've got yourself involved in is very, very dangerous.'

Bert stared into his grandfather's eyes. 'You *are* involved, aren't you?' he said. 'I knew it.'

Heavy footsteps could be heard running towards them down the tunnel.

The gaffer grabbed Bert's hand. 'You must not go back upstairs, Robert. Do you hear me?'

Bert frowned. 'Tonight?'

'Never.'

'But it's my home!' said Bert.

'The people in that meeting – most of them aren't who you think.'

'What?'

'Robert. The real people are dead. They've been

replaced by God knows what. Whatever happens to me, you must not step inside that hotel again.'

'What do you mean, whatever happens to you?'

The gaffer took a note out from the inside of his jacket. He flapped it open and hung it in front of Bert's eyes.

'Who wrote that?' asked Bert. 'The policeman had a note like that, and then he got eaten.'

'I don't know who the letter's from,' said the gaffer. 'But whoever it is, is on to me, Robert. I know too much. It says that I'm the next to go.'

Boom! The battering of the metal door sent shudders across the work surfaces. Vacuum cleaners crashed to the floor.

'Is there another way out of here?' asked Bert, panicking.

Boom! The door was starting to bend and disfigure.

The gaffer pointed towards a rusty ladder against the wall. 'Take the bag,' he said.

'What's in it?'

'Don't ask questions. Just take it.'

Bert heaved the bag on to his back and ran over to the steps. The gaffer, meanwhile, grabbed a metal tap attached to a pipe that wound its way around the room. As he spun the small wheel, a putrid gas billowed from sprinklers in the ceiling.

Boom! The door now had an enormous dent in it and was starting to come away from its hinges.

'What's the gas?'

'Insecticide. Keep climbing,' shouted the gaffer, following him upwards.

'Twistleton?' came the voice from the other side of the door. 'Time to say goodbye, old man.'

Boom!

The steps led up through a small hole in the ceiling, with water cascading down the walls. Bert kept climbing. The ladder was slippery and the strap from his grandfather's bag started to dig into his shoulder.

'Faster,' shouted the gaffer.

'I'm trying.'

With a terrific groaning of metal the door beneath them finally gave way, and a cackling laugh like a hyena's reverberated in Bert's ears.

'You don't think insect repellent's going to stop me, do you, Twistleton?'

Bert climbed up the narrow tunnel. 'I can see a trapdoor above me,' he shouted to his grandfather.

'Reach up and turn it.'

Bert heaved himself up the last few steps and tried to twist the wheel.

'It's rusted over.'

'Try harder.'

Finally, the wheel started to turn, and as he pushed against the door a blast of cool fresh air rushed in through the opening. Poking his head out, Bert recognized the driveway and cars around him. They had come out in the middle of the fountain outside the hotel. In front of him, the enormous floodlit building loomed up into the night sky.

'We're there,' shouted Bert, pulling himself out.

The gaffer climbed out after him and grabbed the bag. 'Come on,' he shouted, wading across the fountain pool with the bag over his shoulder.

They jumped out of the water and ran across the driveway into the tussock grass.

'Get down,' whispered the gaffer.

With his heartbeat thumping in his ears, Bert waited and watched.

Suddenly the shrill ring of a bicycle bell rung out in front of them. It was Ruby speeding towards them out of the darkness.

'Robert! Yoo-hoo.'

'Keep down,' whispered the gaffer to Bert.

'Why are you hiding? I've got something to tell you!'

The gaffer leapt out, grabbed her bike and flung it into the grass, pushing Ruby down after it.

'What the—' started Ruby, before the gaffer pressed his hand across her mouth.

'Look, there it is,' said Bert, as a dark figure, silhouetted against the floodlights, heaved itself out of the top of the fountain. 'It's human,' he whispered, shocked.

'Of course it is,' mouthed the gaffer. 'What did you expect?'

'But *who* is it?'

The figure climbed out and sniffed the air, slowly turning as it spied its surroundings. Suddenly there was laughter as a small group of drunken guests spilt out of the hotel's front doors, singing loudly. The figure grunted, waded through the water and climbed out. With a spit of disgust, it lolloped away down the drive and into the darkness. The gaffer breathed a sigh of relief. Finally he let go of Ruby's mouth.

Furious at being roughly treated, she gasped for air. 'What on earth was all that about?' she hissed.

'Just someone trying to kill us, that's all,' said Bert.

'You could have been in danger,' said the gaffer.

'Thanks for the warning,' she said, not impressed. She sat up and brushed the mud off her coat. 'Anyway, that's exactly what I was coming to tell *you*.'

The gaffer turned his attention from the driveway to Ruby. 'What do you mean?' he said.

Ruby leant over to the basket on the front of her crumpled bike and pulled out the book that she and Bert had taken from the library. 'I've been trying to decipher this,' she said grumpily, tussock grass protruding from her hair in clumps. The gold leaf on the cover sparkled in the hotel lights. 'Turns out this hotel's cursed. Evil, apparently.'

'Don't be so ridiculous, it can't be cursed,' said Bert. 'It's my *home*.'

Ruby stared at Bert, fed up. 'Well, if you don't

believe me we could go and ask the priest, Father
Nathaniel Hooper. He should know.'

Bert and the gaffer frowned. Ruby opened the
book to reveal a portrait of the book's author. Bert
almost choked as the familiar black eyes glared out
of the page.

'He *is* over eight hundred years old, after all.'

Chapter Nine

The Baloddan Princess was a slightly listing rust-bucket of a trawler that had been moored in the harbour for as long as Bert could remember. Now, through the darkness, he could just make out the deck below him, a heaving mass of tangled fishing nets and lobster pots. Hanging precariously over the bow end was a large metal scoop that had once been used for dredging whelks off the sea floor.

'We're going to spend the rest of the night in *that*?' squawked Ruby, hanging over the harbour wall.

Bert looked at his watch. 'Two thirty. Only another three hours till dawn breaks,' he said.

'And only twelve hours or so until the eclipse,'

said the gaffer from the fishing trawler's deck, 'so can we get a move on?'

Bert passed the canvas bag down to his grandfather, and as the moon broke out from behind the clouds, he climbed down on to the boat. Moments later he was joined by Ruby, the priest's book under one arm.

'Right, good,' said the gaffer. 'Follow me.'

He leant over and pulled a rusty chain that hung down beside the mast. With a grating of metal, a trapdoor opened in the floor beside them and they stepped down into the pitch black of the lower deck.

'Here we are,' said the gaffer, striking a match. He lit a gas lamp on a ledge beside him, and as the wick flared Bert and Ruby gawped at their surroundings.

'Welcome to my little hide-away,' he said, grinning.

They were standing in a decadently furnished study. There were oriental rugs covering the floor, old garden chairs with cushions gathered around a table, a hammock suspended from the wrought iron ceiling, and maps, compasses and pencils spread out across the table. It looked more like a hotel room than the lower deck of a fishing trawler.

'Blimey,' said Ruby, utterly gobsmacked.

'I thought this boat was derelict,' said Bert.

The gaffer grinned. 'That's the intention,' he said. 'Tea?' Ruby nodded. The gaffer walked over to a sink in the corner and filled a kettle.

'So how long have you had this place?' asked Bert, giving the hammock a swing.

'Oh, a few years,' said the gaffer. 'I made it as a bolthole. For when it became too dangerous to stay up at the hotel.' He turned round to face them. 'And now that time's arrived. Sugar?'

Ruby frowned. 'You *knew* you'd have to leave the hotel?' she asked, sitting down at the table.

'I've known for a long time.'

Bert sat down beside Ruby, clutching his head as he tried to take everything in. 'So how long exactly have you known what was going on at the hotel?' he asked. 'Months? Years even?'

'I've had inklings that something odd was going on since I was a boy.'

'You've kept this quiet for over seventy years?' spluttered Bert.

'When my father built the hotel,' the gaffer continued, 'over the monastery ruins as it turned out, we found piles of ancient manuscripts and maps. We uncovered tunnels where we found paintings of the solar eclipse. The pictures were all very bloody and unnerving, and there were lines and lines of Roman numerals carved into the walls. Mediaeval, we thought. My father had them bricked up and then built over. He said it was a load of superstitious nonsense.'

'And what happened to your father?' asked Ruby, peering at one of the maps.

'A building accident,' said the gaffer.

Suddenly the shrill whistle of the kettle blew, like a child's piercing scream.

'So did you know that people were disappearing back then?' asked Bert. 'Like the librarian?'

The gaffer filled the mugs, sat down and handed one of them to Ruby.

'There'd always been gossip of people disappearing. It'd been talked about for years. Behind closed doors of course. Meanwhile I met your grandmother at a local dance. Well, she found me to be precise. We courted and she asked me to marry her. She was quite a woman, your grandmother.' The gaffer smiled gently. 'Your father was born and I built up the hotel. We were happy. I was busy. But still I spent my spare time recording all the strange deaths that were taking place in and around Baloddan.'

'The photographs in the room beside your bedroom?' said Bert excitedly.

'Yes,' said the gaffer.

'Like the one of my aunt,' said Ruby slowly.

'Yes,' said the gaffer again. 'I began to suspect there was something lurking in the tunnels under the hotel that was taking them. Eating them. I'd find evidence of the struggles. I'd hear the screams.'

Ruby turned pale.

'So did you *know* what it was?' Bert asked the gaffer. 'Did you ever see what was taking them?'

'No.' The gaffer took a slurp of tea. 'I never saw it.

I heard it, I think. Howling in the night. But then, when I investigated further, I found that whoever I *thought* had been taken would shortly appear again. Alive and healthy. As if they'd never died at all.' The gaffer paused. 'But of course it wasn't them.'

'It wasn't?' asked Bert.

The gaffer picked up the priest's book. 'They were replicas,' he said. 'Brilliant replicas, perfect in every detail.'

'And according to this book of the priest's,' said Ruby, '*worshippers* of some kind.'

'Like a continuation of that weird monastery, then?' said Bert.

'According to Father Hooper's account, they've come to witness the release of a beast,' said Ruby. 'It's all in the book, like it's history repeating itself eight hundred years after the last solar eclipse. And last time the place got looted and destroyed. The monastery was levelled.'

Bert sat there, stunned. 'So, didn't you ever think of telling someone all this?' he asked his grandfather.

'I started to receive mysterious letters warning me off. They threatened my family, said I'd be involved in a nasty accident if I told anyone. Which is why I spent so much time in hiding.'

'But why weren't you taken like all the others? Like my aunt,' asked Ruby. 'Why were you just warned? What made *you* so special?'

The gaffer suddenly looked down at the table. He

mumbled while Bert and Ruby waited for an answer. His vice-like grip around his mug of tea was growing stronger. The blood was draining from his knuckles.

'And you never seemed sad when Granny died,' said Bert quietly. 'I never understood why you weren't sad like the rest of us.'

'Who was warning you?' asked Ruby.

Suddenly Bert's grandfather turned and glared at them. His face was white, and his eyes bloodshot with anger. 'Enough questions,' he said. 'Enough. That's it.'

Bert had never seen his grandfather react so sharply. Ruby didn't know where to look.

Suddenly the gaffer's head fell into his hands. 'It's all my fault,' he whispered. 'I'm sorry. Everything's my fault.'

'I don't understand, Grandpa . . .' began Bert, but Ruby grabbed his arm. She shook her head.

'Don't push him,' she whispered.

'Look, we've only got a few hours to stop whatever's underneath that hotel,' said Bert.

'And we'll get eaten if we try,' said Ruby. 'You've heard the warnings.'

'So we get rid of whoever's writing these letters first, this *protector*,' said Bert. 'Then we go for the beast thing.'

'Do you think the protector's Hooper?' asked Ruby.

The gaffer looked up. His eyes looked raw. 'Your

grandmother never trusted Hooper. She loathed him even. He never seemed to age for one thing.' He took another slurp of his tea. 'But eight hundred years old or not, he never struck me as a *bad* man.'

'He's all we've got,' said Bert. 'If he's the one, he's protecting something very old, very evil and plainly very dangerous. Follow him and I bet we find the creature.'

The gaffer looked up. 'If he *is* the one, he'll kill you first.'

'The whole thing rests on *my* shoulders now?' asked Bert.

'I'm too old for this game, Robert,' said the gaffer.

'*I'm* coming with you though,' said Ruby, standing bolt upright.

'It's your destiny, Robert. And they won't be expecting you to do anything,' said the gaffer. 'They're expecting *me*.'

'But . . .' stuttered Bert. 'If it *is* up to us . . . and if we *do* get past whoever's *protecting* it, and we do eventually uncover this evil monster thing . . . how do we stop it before it eats us? Am I supposed to wrestle with it?'

'Oh no, you won't need to wrestle with it,' said the gaffer, heaving the giant canvas bag slowly on to the table. Bert watched as his grandfather patted it lovingly. 'This baby'll deal with that.'

* * *

As dawn broke over the village roofs, and the fishing trawlers chugged their way into the harbour with the morning's catch, Bert, Ruby and the gaffer braced themselves for the day ahead.

'Here,' said the gaffer, lobbing a heavy-looking two-way radio across the room.

Bert caught it and turned it over in his hands. 'Does it work?' he said, yawning.

'Should do,' said the gaffer. 'I made it.'

Bert twisted the knob by the aerial. The radio crackled and hissed angrily.

'Ruby, I want to know every move the two of you make,' said the gaffer. 'Keep a low profile and keep me updated. They'll be waiting for us.'

Ruby nodded.

'So we're agreed. It's to Hooper's house first?' asked Bert, peering out of a porthole.

The gaffer nodded. 'Keep out of sight, and hopefully he'll lead us straight to whatever's hiding under that hotel.'

'And where'll you be?' asked Ruby.

'I won't be far away,' said the gaffer.

'What happens when and if we find this thing?' asked Bert.

The gaffer turned to them. 'We'll cross that bridge when we come to it,' he said.

Pushing open the trapdoor, Bert and Ruby climbed out into the daylight. The gaffer watched them as they stepped off the boat and on to the pavement, the ladder now having disappeared under several feet of water. Bert turned and waved to his grandfather.

'Good luck, Robert,' said the gaffer. 'And be careful.'

Bert nodded nervously and the gaffer closed the hatch.

Baloddan had changed considerably in the last couple of days. Large banners crossed the streets and swathes of bunting hung between the lampposts. In a few hours the village would be bristling with noisy visitors streaming in and out of the shops, laden with brightly coloured sticks of rock and ice creams. For the moment, though, all was quiet save the trawlermen heaving their catch on to the harbour wall.

'The calm before the storm,' said Ruby anxiously as they walked past the row of shops.

Bert looked at his watch. It was almost six. 'Come on,' he said, breaking into a jog. 'We'd better get to Hooper's house.'

As they ran over the cobbles and turned up into the maze of streets that led away from the water's edge, a curtain twitched in the window of the grocery store. A cat jumped up on to the windowsill and rubbed itself along the glass, as a dark pair of eyes watched Bert and Ruby disappear out of sight.

* * *

'We've arrived,' said Bert into the radio mouthpiece, as he and Ruby squatted in the doorway of the building opposite.

Father Hooper's house, much like the village library in the next-door street, was one of a row of small, beamed houses attached on both sides. The building leant precariously down towards the harbour, and the upper storey hung out over the cobbled street below. The house to its right was boarded up and looked like it had been uninhabited for years.

'Any signs of Hooper?' crackled the gaffer's voice over the airwaves.

'Not yet,' whispered Bert. 'The curtains are still closed and two fresh milk bottles are sitting outside the front door.'

Suddenly Ruby prodded Bert in the ribs.

'Hang on,' whispered Bert.

The curtains had been opened in the upstairs window. They could clearly see Hooper peering out and then disappearing from sight.

'He's in there,' said Bert.

The radio whistled.

'Keep watching him,' said the gaffer. 'If he moves, follow him.'

'Will do.'

Bert attached the radio to his belt.

'We sit here,' he said to Ruby, 'until he leaves the house.'

Two hours passed uneventfully. The curtains to the downstairs window remained closed and the milk bottles untouched. Upstairs, the priest would occasionally appear in the window, pacing manically to and fro. His hair looked wild, as if he'd just got out of bed.

'Weirdo,' muttered Bert, yawning. The exhaustion of the past few hours was beginning to catch up with him and, although his bottom was feeling numb from sitting on the stones, he began to nod off.

'Oi!' whispered Ruby, grabbing his shoulder.

A small lady, dressed in a blue pinafore and thick black tights, had turned up at the door. Her hair was tied up in a bun and she was singing cheerfully to herself as she pulled the house keys from her pocket.

Bert rubbed his eyes. 'It's only the charlady,' he said, scratching his back on the brickwork behind him.

The woman opened the door and wobbled inside.

'Morning, Father Hooper,' she called in a strange accent. She waited, listening for a second, and then closed the door behind her. Bert closed his eyes again and started to drift off.

'AAAAAAAARGHH!' came a sudden scream from the other side of the front door. Bert almost fell over as Ruby jumped to her feet. Hooper's door burst open and the cleaning lady ran out into the street shrieking at the top of her voice. Ruby ran out to the old lady and Bert hurriedly switched on the radio.

'Grandpa? Grandpa! Are you there?'

The radio remained silent. Then, suddenly, it crackled to life.

'Here. Radio . . . playing up. What is it?' came the disjointed voice of the gaffer.

'Something's happened inside the house,' replied Bert.

Ruby was trying to hold on to the old woman as she struggled to get away.

'Grandpa? Can you hear me?'

The radio hissed and crackled, but the gaffer didn't reply. The old lady pulled herself free and ran down the street screaming. Up and down the street, people were starting to look out of their doors.

Bert ran over to join Ruby. 'What did she say?' he asked.

'Not sure,' said Ruby. 'My Spanish isn't up to much.'

'Let's go inside,' said Bert, scurrying towards the house, 'before someone starts to ask questions.'

'But your grandfather told us to stay put.'

Bert fiddled with the knob on the radio.

'Grandpa? Can you hear me?' The radio crackled and popped. Bert shook it and then shoved it in his pocket. 'Homemade piece of junk,' he spat. 'Come on. My decision. We're going in.'

'But . . .'

Bert twisted the door handle and pushed open the creaking door. He was immediately hit by the most appalling stench, a smell so sharp he found himself almost gagging. Stumbling backwards out into the daylight, he gasped for air.

'Crikey,' he choked, his eyes streaming. 'It's that damn insect repellent again.'

Ruby took a hanky out of her jeans pocket and pressed it against her nose. She leant forward and peered into the house. 'Oh. My. Goodness,' she said. She turned round to face Bert. 'Have you seen inside?'

Bert straightencd himself, took a big gulp of clean air and peered in. The front hall had been ransacked. Pictures had been torn off the wall, the carpet had been pulled up, vases and lamps had been smashed on the ground, and graffiti had been splashed and scrawled over every surface.

'Jeez,' said Bert, holding on to his nose. 'Subwud's god wild id here.'

Ruby stepped in and hoiked open a window. 'Father?' she called up the stairs.

Bert glared at her. 'What are you doing?' he hissed.

'We've got to make sure he's all right. His home's been burgled.' Ruby called up the stairs again. 'Father Hooper?'

The house remained silent. Bert looked around

136

and then read the graffiti on the walls. '*Metuite.*
Belua resurget.'

'It's the same eclipse warnings as down in the
tunnels,' said Ruby. 'And the Roman numerals, over
and over again.'

Bert touched the paint. It was still wet.

'Who do you think did it?' he asked.

Ruby shrugged and walked through into the sitting
room. 'Take a look at this!' she gasped.

Bert joined her only to be met with yet more
destruction. Tables had been turned over and
cabinets torn off the walls. The floor was a carpet
of burning candles and the graffiti was everywhere,
on the floor, ceiling, even on the overturned
furniture.

'It looks like someone's gone totally insane,' said
Bert.

'Looks like *Hooper's* gone totally insane, I think,'
said Ruby.

Suddenly the radio in Bert's pocket started to pop
and whistle. He pulled it out.

'Robert? Ruby?' came the familiar voice of the
gaffer.

Bert pressed the talk button with his thumb.
'You're not going to believe this,' he said.

'Has the priest gone?' asked the gaffer frantically.
He sounded in a panic.

Bert stuck his head through into the tiny kitchen.
'Yes. I think so. But . . . how did you guess?'

'There must be a tunnel opening in his house. Find it,' said the gaffer. 'It's important. We can't lose him.'

'Grandpa, are you all right?' asked Bert, worried. 'Where are you?'

'Something's turned up, Robert. There's things I should have told you. Things I should have told you years ago.'

'Bert!' shouted Ruby from upstairs. 'Come and look what I've found.'

Bert ran up the stairs into the priest's ransacked bedroom. Ruby was studying the fireplace, where a trail of paint led straight into the hearth of the fire and stopped dead against the back wall.

'Hmm,' said Bert. 'I wonder if this is the opening?'

He kicked the grate. Suddenly, with an ominous groan as if the whole building was about to fall down, the wall in front of them slid away, revealing a hole into the adjoining building. The graffiti continued for as far as the eye could see.

'I think we've just found that tunnel you were after,' said Bert into the radio mouthpiece. The radio whistled.

'Always come prepared,' said Ruby, pulling out a small torch from her pocket.

'What haven't you told me, Grandpa?' asked Bert frantically into the radio. 'Is there something Ruby and I need to know? What's so important?'

The radio whistled and hissed.

'Watch your back, Robert . . . Hooper . . . not who . . . may think . . . booby traps . . .'

'Grandpa?' Bert shouted.

Silence. And then one last distinct word.

'Cats.'

'Grandpa?' said Bert. 'Grandpa?' he shouted.

The radio popped and whistled.

'Robert?' asked Ruby. Bert looked up at her. 'What did he tell you?'

The radio went dead. Bert frowned.

'I'm not sure,' he said.

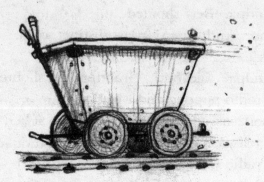

Chapter Ten

Ruby shone the torch beam through the hole in the fireplace and into the next-door house. Strange objects glistened inside, sparkling like jewels.

'This must be the place that was boarded up,' she whispered.

Bert leant in. The air was thick with insect repellent fumes, and a faint glow of daylight came from a blacked-out window on the other side of the room.

'Hand me the torch a moment,' said Bert. 'There's something in here.'

Ruby handed the flashlight over and Bert stepped through the hole. The floorboards creaked under his weight. As he waved the beam around in the darkness, the light reflected off a huge collection of golden ornaments and furniture, sending rainbows of colour spilling across the room.

'It's full of antiques,' said Ruby.

'It's full of *something*,' said Bert.

The walls were covered with paintings, some of them clearly hundreds of years old. There were golden icons, statues, crosses studded with gemstones, all stacked up against each other. And up against the far wall stood a vast lectern with a majestic golden eagle glaring out.

'The ransacked monastery,' gasped Bert to himself.

'The *what*?' asked Ruby, stepping through to join him. Bert spun round.

'Didn't that book say the monastery was ransacked and burnt down after the last eclipse?'

'Erm, yes. I think so, but that was in 1234.'

'Well, this must be what's left of the ornaments. This is what the priest managed to save,' said Bert, excitedly, 'from the looters.'

Ruby picked up a heavy-looking orb, its glimmering gold surface embedded with jewels. 'But this lot must be priceless,' she spluttered. 'There's tons of it. Hooper can't have carried it out on his own, it would have taken him years.'

Bert ran his finger along the frame of one of the pictures, scraping up layers of dust. 'He could have hidden it first,' he said, 'and then brought it here gradually, piece by piece.'

'But wouldn't people have seen him with it?' asked Ruby. 'You can't carry this lot into a busy village without being seen.'

Bert smiled. 'Unless you bring it underground,' he said.

'What?'

'Through a tunnel. We know this area's full of them.'

'Robert, I hope you're not thinking of leading me down another dangerous tunnel.'

'Wouldn't dream of it,' said Bert, shining the torch beam on to the ground. The streaming red paint that had led them to the fireplace next door was now strewn across the floorboards. Bert followed the path to the top of a rickety staircase in the corner of the room and peered down into the blackness.

'I knew I shouldn't have got involved in this,' said Ruby, anxiously.

'Come on.' Bert stepped down on to the top stair. The boards groaned underneath him. 'It's fine,' he said, trying to reassure her. 'Really it is.'

Suddenly the stair splintered and broke under his weight. He tried to grab the banister, but with another crack the stair collapsed and Bert dropped down into the darkness. With deafening thuds and cracks as he hit each step, he crashed down the staircase. The torch cartwheeled after him, shooting arcs of light in all directions, until it smacked against the wall and went out. With a final thud, Bert reached the base of the stairwell.

'Robert?' came Ruby's panicked voice from way above him. He'd obviously fallen quite a way. Disorientated and sore, he tried to lift his head. He was resting up against a hard wall, his arms twisted beneath him.

'Robert? Answer me, Robert? Are you OK?'

Bert could hear the clumping of Ruby's footsteps reverberating in his ears as she tried to make her way down the stairs towards him.

'Just be careful,' groaned Bert, his head spinning. 'Some of those steps are rotten.'

He pulled his arm out from under him, fumbled for the torch and flicked it on. The beam glowed weakly.

'I told you. This place is falling apart around us,' Ruby said, straining to pull Bert to his feet. 'It's too dangerous. We've got to go back.'

'No chance,' said Bert, rubbing his neck. His back ached and he'd ripped his jumper. 'We haven't come this far to give up now.' He waved the torch beam around, trying to find out where he'd landed.

Ruby looked up, and promptly dropped Bert back on to the ground. 'Jeez,' she said.

Bert had landed on a wooden platform in a long, narrow tunnel that had been carved out of the stone. He'd hit his head on a small but heavy-looking cart the size of a bath, with iron wheels resting on a track that led off into the darkness.

'Where on earth does that go?' asked Ruby.

Bert had managed to get up again, and was now rubbing his grazed forehead. 'Haven't a clue,' he said. 'But I have a funny idea that Hooper's not far away. This is how he must have transported all that monastery stuff.'

'I don't like this, Robert,' said Ruby, suddenly taking a step back towards the stairs. 'This place is booby-trapped.'

'Nonsense,' said Bert, examining the wagon.

Suddenly they heard a gentle creak of a floorboard above them. A faint light appeared at the top of the stairs as another torch beam was waved around the room. Bert grabbed Ruby and pulled her out of view.

'The light!' he whispered, fumbling for the flashlight. With a click he turned it out.

'There's someone else in the house,' said Bert.

Standing in the pitch darkness Ruby began to shake uncontrollably. 'Who?' she asked.

'Hooper probably.'

'But the house was empty,' said Ruby.

'We didn't check every room,' said Bert.

The footsteps crossed the floor above them and a beam of light shone directly down the staircase, catching the toe of Ruby's shoe. Bert could hear somebody sniffing, smelling the air like a wild animal. A quiet rumble of laughter shook the stairs.

'We're dead,' whispered Ruby, squeezing Bert's hand as she started to quietly sob in terror.

Slowly, tentatively they heard a step creak as whoever was above them began to descend the staircase.

'On the count of three,' whispered Bert, 'we jump in the cart.'

'Are you mad? I can't move,' said Ruby.

'No choice. One.'

'Robert.'

'Two.'

'I can't do it.'

'Three.'

Bert leapt for the cart, pushing Ruby in front of him. As Ruby toppled inside, Bert gave the wagon an almighty shove and jumped in after her. The cart rolled into the darkness as they heard the heavy clatter of footsteps and an almighty thud as a body landed on the platform behind them. Suddenly a blinding beam was shone directly down the tunnel, dazzling Bert and hiding the figure behind it. Bert ducked underneath the rim of the wagon, as it quickly began to gather pace.

'Was it Hooper?' asked Ruby, not daring to look back.

'I don't know,' said Bert, panting.

Suddenly an ear-splitting scream, like a howling animal, reverberated down the track, sending shivers down Bert's spine.

'And I'm not sure I want to find out,' he said.

The cart began to jerk and rattle as it gathered momentum, the track chattering beneath them.

'Can he follow us?' asked Ruby.

'Probably,' said Bert. 'But he'll take a while. We've got the only cart.'

The wagon sped through the tunnel like a rollercoaster, throwing its occupants from side to side as it hurtled round the bends. Bert and Ruby held on for dear life as the cart ducked, dived and wove through the twisting tunnel, the ceiling only inches above their heads.

'Do you have any idea where this leads?' asked Ruby over the roar of the wheels.

'Haven't a clue,' replied Bert. 'Let's just hope it's not towards the cliffs.'

Ruby shot back a look of renewed panic.

'Only kidding,' said Bert.

On and on the cart sped, the track rattling underneath them as they careered through the underground passage.

'When's this thing going to stop?' asked Ruby.

Suddenly there was an almighty crash as the cart slammed to a halt, winding Bert and Ruby with the force of the collision. Fighting for breath, Bert pulled himself up, slipped over the edge of the wagon and landed in a heap on the ground.

'Robert?' came Ruby's weak voice. 'Are you all right?'

Bert opened his eyes. The tunnel was lighter now,

with burning torches in the walls. He saw that the cart had collided with a row of others, all lined up against a buffer where the tunnel came to an end.

'I think I've had enough of being thrown around for one day,' said Bert.

Ruby pulled herself out of the wagon and on to the platform. She had a cut to her ear which was bleeding badly. Bert stumbled to his feet.

'Do you think that thing's still after us?' she said, peering back into the darkness.

'I don't think we should hang around to find out.'

'But where are we?' asked Ruby.

Bert looked around him. Faintly, in the distance, he could hear a chanting noise, a single voice muttering. A small doorway stood at the end of the tunnel. Bert limped towards it. 'There's only one way to find out,' he whispered. He turned the handle, opened the door, and stepped in.

'Twistleton! Pah!' came a harsh, familiar voice. 'I should have guessed he'd send a child for me.'

Ruby looked over Bert's shoulder at a strange figure peering at them. 'Father Hooper?' she asked.

There, huddled in the murk of a small room sat Father Nathaniel Hooper, naked apart from a pair of filthy underpants, and covered from head to foot in painted numbers. His black hair stuck out of his head as if an electric current was running through it, and he rocked to and fro on his heels chanting and muttering like a crazed lunatic.

'What's he saying?' whispered Ruby into Bert's ear. 'He looks completely mad.'

The priest got to his feet and lit the wick of a lantern, illuminating the small hexagonal room around them. Fresh wet paint was spewed over the floor and graffiti covered the walls. He hopped towards them like a slimy toad.

'I live in this hell-hole of a village for over eight hundred years,' he jabbered, 'and he thinks I'll spill my secret to a *child*. Ignorant fool.'

'What's he mumbling about?' asked Ruby.

But Bert was too busy examining the room around them. He had the feeling he'd seen it before. He was convinced he'd *been* in it before. Suddenly he clicked.

'We're in the vault, Ruby,' he whispered. Ruby frowned. 'The vault we fell in! By the old chapel, next door to the vestry.'

Suddenly the priest jumped up off the floor and eyeballed Bert, his putrid, stale breath almost making Bert throw up.

'I've got what he needs to let the beast free,' giggled the priest, almost childlike in his excitement. 'He can't let it free without my help!'

Bert tried to pull his face away as the priest hooted with laughter.

'*He?* Who's *he*?' asked Bert, grimacing. He could hardly hear what the priest was saying, let alone understand him.

'And now he sends you to *prod* and *cajole* me,' whispered Hooper, jabbing Bert in the chest with a long, bony finger. 'He sends you, a pathetic *child*, to make me talk.' He waggled his long, slimy tongue in front of Bert's eyes. 'I always knew you were one of them, Robert Twistleton.'

'But I'm trying to help,' said Bert, bewildered.

The priest eyeballed him, then dropped back to the floor. 'Trying to help,' he mumbled with contempt. 'Pah!'

Ruby had had enough. 'Robert, let's find a way out of here. He's a mad, dribbling old fool babbling a whole load of useless nonsense. This eclipse thing has plainly driven him nuts.'

Ruby turned back and headed for the door.

'Wait!' said Bert, watching the priest as he crawled around the edge of the room, muttering to himself.

'He's not mad, he's terrified,' said Bert. 'He's eight hundred years old and terrified. If he really has got what's needed to let that creature out, then whoever was back there definitely wasn't after *us*. They've come to get *him*.'

'Robert, I don't care how old he is or what he's hiding. If we hang around much longer we're all goners.'

Bert took Ruby by the shoulders. 'Ruby. This is what we've come for. It's up to us. We must find out what's going on.'

'Whoever's behind us has threatened your grandfather, sent the priest here crazy, and probably killed half the village. I'm not sure *I* want to hang around to join them.' She turned round to the door.

'Ruby!'

Suddenly, with a thundering crash, the door in front of her burst off its hinges and flew into the room, knocking Ruby clean off her feet. As she slumped to the ground like a dead weight, a plague of cats surged through the open doorway and into the vault. There were ginger cats, black cats, albinos. Bert was pushed back against the far wall by the sheer weight of numbers. And slowly a small, bent over figure, holding a burning torch in one hand, stepped in through the doorway.

'Whicker,' gasped Bert.

The shopkeeper flashed an evil grin.

'Miaow,' he said.

Bent over and shuffling, Whicker slowly circled the vault, the flaming torch in his hand filling the room with a deep orange glow. Only now could Bert see the true magnificence of the ornate carvings and paintings on the walls around him. The room was truly beautiful.

'Father Hooper,' wheezed Mr Whicker in his high-pitched voice, his limbs and head twitching spasmodically like an insect, 'what a pleasant surprise.'

Paralysed with fear, Bert watched the priest as he cowered on the far side of the room. Ruby, meanwhile, was still lying motionless in a heap on the floor.

'I suppose you know what I've come for, Hooper?' said the grocer. The priest looked up and spat at him. 'You pathetic leech,' growled Whicker, wiping the spittle from his face. He lunged at the priest, picking him up like a rag doll.

Frightened what Whicker would do next, Bert desperately thought of something to say. 'Are you the one who sent the death threats to my grandfather?' he spluttered, over the noise of the cats.

Shocked, Whicker flicked his gaze towards Bert. 'How sweet,' he croaked, dropping Father Hooper to the ground. 'What a caring grandson you are.'

'And the note to the policeman? You sent that too,' said Bert, shaking with fear.

'Yes. Just before he was eaten.'

The priest turned to Bert and feebly tried to get to his feet. 'Don't speak to him!' he said. 'Don't give him the pleasure.'

'Shut up, you snivelling fool!' spat Mr Whicker in a burst of anger, and he kicked the priest back down to the ground.

Terrified, Bert edged around the room, Mr Whicker and the plague of cats following his every step.

'So you're the protector? The one that's been shielding this beast?' asked Bert, nervously. 'You allowed all those innocent people to die? Like my grandmother.'

'Oh come, come,' said Whicker. 'So much hatred isn't healthy for a small boy.'

'He's the keeper of the beast!' shouted the priest. 'The curse of Baloddan.'

Bert glared at Hooper. 'Baloddan's cursed?'

'Not really a curse,' said Whicker smiling, 'more of a blessing. A line of creatures, my angels, each one human in its pupae years, that reaches full maturity at the eclipse when its metamorphosis is finished. Then its true beauty is finally revealed.'

'And the feeding frenzy starts,' said the priest.

Bert felt confused. 'And you protect this *thing* from harm before the eclipse?' he asked.

'Call me a doting nanny if you will,' said Whicker, chuckling. 'A sort of zoo keeper.'

'He's thousands of years old,' said the priest. 'Evil itself. He's the Devil incarnate!'

Whicker's eyes flashed with anger as he turned round and unleashed a second kick to the priest, sending him sliding across the floor.

'Quiet, imbecile!'

The priest lay hunched up and whimpering. 'We built the monastery in 1180,' he moaned, determined to keep talking, 'above the old tunnels that wove their way under the cliffs, where the creature was said to lurk. But we were powerless against this sort of evil and soon the monks started changing around me. They were being eaten.'

'We were building a *new* following,' said Whicker, smiling proudly.

'A few of us could see what was happening. So we torched the monastery at the eclipse in 1234, killing the beast and its followers.'

'We found the diary you wrote,' said Bert.

Whicker mockingly wiped a tear from his eye.

The priest continued. 'But we knew that we hadn't got rid of the bloodline completely,' he said feebly. 'We suspected that Whicker here was nurturing another monster. We didn't know who or where it was, so we placed a curse on Whicker . . .'

'Hardly a curse,' laughed Whicker. 'More an inconvenience.'

'. . . so that we always knew when he was close by. It was all we could do. He was too powerful.'

Bert frowned.

'Cats,' said the priest. 'Noisy cats.'

'Feline vermin!' screamed Whicker, picking a fat ginger up by the scruff of its neck. The cat hissed and spat in his face. 'Stinking, mewing, creeping vermin. I've tried to ignore them for eight hundred years, but they get under your skin. Miaow. They start getting inside your head. Miaow. God, how I hate cats!'

Bert flinched as Whicker threw the cat, howling, at the wall.

'And now I get my revenge,' growled Whicker, his anger rising. 'I keep old man Hooper here alive so that he can bear witness, powerless in his old age, to the oncoming carnage.'

'While the hotel becomes a feeding ground,' said Bert.

Whicker flashed a menacing grin. 'Just a little hors d'oeuvre,' he chuckled, rubbing his hands together with glee, 'before the real fun starts.'

'And that's why you've been printing all those posters. The hotel's a trap, to entice people to the area as a source of food?'

Whicker started to laugh. 'Don't blame it all on me,' he chuckled. '*I* didn't build the place!'

Bert felt confused. Lost. Angry.

Suddenly the priest spoke up. 'But none of this can happen before you find the key, Whicker,' he said.

Mr Whicker marched over to the priest, stooped down and pulled him to his feet. 'Oh yes. The key.'

'The monks had a key to the tunnels,' shouted Father Hooper to Bert.

'Another of their little jokes,' said Whicker sarcastically, jabbing Hooper in the ribs.

'There's only one way that monster can get out, now it will have grown so big. And we made a key to the exit, right under Whicker's nose.'

'And now I've come to find where this key is,' said Whicker jovially. 'Before I *kill* you.'

'I'll never tell you.'

Whicker threw the priest to the ground.

'You don't *need* to tell me,' he howled, 'now young Mr Twistleton here has so kindly led me to your little hidey-hole. The answer lies here in this room. Inscribed in these walls for the past seven centuries. Correct?'

The priest didn't flinch.

Whicker smiled again. 'Thought so,' he said.

Bert watched the evil grocer as he slowly circled the room, examining the walls with the burning torch held high over his head. As he muttered to himself, translating the reams of Latin in front of him, the plague of cats followed his every move, rubbing themselves against his calves.

But as Bert watched Whicker, wondering what he'd have to do to stop him, he spotted Ruby winking at him from the centre of the room. She must have been awake all the time.

'It's underneath me,' she mouthed silently.

Whicker's ears twitched.

'The answer.'

Bert frowned as Ruby pointed to the floor beneath where she lay.

Suddenly Whicker spun round and stared at Ruby. 'Get up,' he spat.

Ruby played dead.

'Get up! I know you can hear me. What do you think I am, some old cretinous fool?'

He picked Ruby up, and threw her against the wall beside Bert.

'You think I'm human, don't you? You think I can't hear you, can't see you, can't smell your every move?'

He got down on his hands and knees, bringing the flame right down to the floor. The ground was a landscape of carved writing, pictures and inscriptions. And there, right in the centre, was a simple, short sentence.

'The key shall directly oppose he who seeks it,' translated Whicker. He spun round and glared at the priest. His eyes had started to glow red like hot coals, and his skin was bubbling and steaming. 'What does this mean?' he asked quietly.

The priest looked away.

'WHAT DOES THIS MEAN?' Whicker screamed again. He got up, picked Father Hooper up by the leg and dragged him into the air, as if he was as light as a feather. 'What does this mean, Hooper?' he growled, his voice shaking the walls around the vault.

'Kill me,' screamed the priest. 'I'll never tell you.'

Whicker hurled Father Hooper across the room.

'You will tell me, Hooper. TELL ME.'

Rocks and earth from the ceiling started to fall to the ground as the room shook. Again Whicker went to pick Hooper up, this time by his hair.

'You'll regret the day you were born, Hooper, if you don't tell me where the key is.'

Suddenly, on the other side of the room, Bert

glared at Ruby. He had an idea he knew what this was all about. 'Who can you think of that dislikes Whicker,' he whispered.

Ruby shook her head. 'Your grandfather?' she said. 'But he can't have the key.'

'No, I mean someone who can't *bear* him.'

'How about Mr Dawbany? Father Hooper? Us?'

'No, someone who can't be in the same room as him.' He watched Whicker shaking the priest violently on the other side of the room. 'Someone who Whicker himself really detests. Someone who he fights with, like cat and—' Bert stopped.

'What?' asked Ruby.

'Oh my God,' whispered Bert suddenly. 'We're not looking for a key at all. Not even a person.'

'*What?*'

'We're looking for a dog. Dawbany's pug dog. Elvis opposes Whicker at every possible moment. The key's a dog.'

Suddenly the grocer dropped Father Hooper to the ground and looked back over his shoulder.

'Oh, Twistleton,' he said, smiling. He stepped towards Bert. 'And to think I tried to frighten you off under the kitchens. You *do* have your uses, just like your pathetic grandfather.' Bert began to back away. 'So, it's the pug dog, is it? Of course, how ingenious.' He leant down to Bert's face and flicked a lizard-like tongue out, licking Bert's cheek. 'Thank you,' he said softly in Bert's ear.

Suddenly he hurled his burning torch down at the smashed wooden door on the ground, causing the flames to flare up and fill the doorway to the tunnel. He leapt into the air and hung off the ceiling like a fly, lifting the stone ceiling above him. The gravestone which Ruby and Bert had fallen through rose and sunlight burst into the room.

'By the time you get out of here,' he cackled, '*if* you ever get out of here, my job shall be done.'

As he jumped up through the hole, the cats on the vault floor miaowed and hissed, desperate to follow.

Whicker smiled. 'Goodbye,' he said, and he dragged the stone back after him, leaving Bert, Ruby and the priest behind in the burning room. The priest stared at the ceiling in desperation. Slowly he looked up at Bert and Ruby, who'd both slumped to the floor.

'We've lost,' he said feebly. 'The village is doomed.'

Chapter Eleven

With flames licking the walls and ceiling, and thick smoke swirling overhead, Bert, Ruby and the priest retreated to the far wall of the vault, away from the intense heat of the fire. The opening to the tunnel that led back to the village had collapsed, and with it the chances of escaping were fast diminishing.

'We've got to find a way out of here,' panicked Ruby, her face bright pink from the heat, 'before this whole room caves in on top of us.'

Bert was carefully looking around him. 'That door we found to the vestry,' he said, 'it can't have just disappeared.'

'It should be easy to find now we can see,' said Ruby.

They both examined the granite walls of the ancient vault. Heavily inscribed with a forest of carved letters and strewn with fresh red paint, there was no sign of a doorway anywhere.

'It must be here,' called Bert above the roar of the fire.

Ruby looked up at the priest. His face, covered in warpaint, seemed more wrinkled now, his eyes more sallow and drawn as he stared trance-like into the flames.

'Father Hooper,' she said. 'Please help us. The corridor that leads to the vestry, we need you to tell us how to get to it.'

The priest turned and looked at Ruby, his gaze penetrating deep into her eyes. 'Leaving is futile,' he said wistfully. 'The end has finally come. The beast shall be let loose. It is time to accept our destiny.'

Bert grabbed the priest's arm. 'Oh no, we're not giving up just yet. We can still stop this thing. You must tell us where the door is.'

Father Hooper smiled and slowly shook his head. '*Futura in manibus tuis sunt*,' he said softly, staring back into the flames. '*Futura in manibus tuis sunt*.'

'He's gone mad,' said Bert, running his hands desperately over the wall. 'We'll have to find it ourselves.'

'No, wait,' said Ruby. 'He's telling us something.'

The priest raised his arms towards the fire. '*Futura in manibus tuis sunt,*' he chanted.

'We haven't got time for this rubbish, Ruby,' choked Bert.

Ruby was thinking hard. *Futura in manibus* . . . I must know this,' she muttered. 'The . . . *futura* . . . future . . . is . . . in . . .' Suddenly she spun round and glared at the carved writing. 'It's on the wall!' she said. 'What he's saying's on the wall.'

'How do you know?' asked Bert.

'Just find the words and I'll explain.'

'*Futura in manibus* . . .' chanted the priest, now rocking to and fro on his heels.

With his eyes stinging from the smoke, Bert tried to focus on the swirling mass of letters carved in front of him. 'Well if the words are here, then I can't see them!' he said.

'Keep looking,' said Ruby. 'They *must* be here.'

Suddenly, like a vision, the words appeared in front of Bert's eyes, a single sentence carefully hidden amongst the forest of carved letters.

' "*Futura in manibus tuis sunt* . . ." I've got it!' He looked back to Ruby. 'I've got it, look.'

Ruby bent down and studied the words closely.

'Now what?' asked Bert, keeping an eye on the advancing flames.

'Now we open the door,' said Ruby and she ran her hand over the letters.

'*Futura in* manibus . . .'

As if out of nowhere she felt and picked out an iron door handle so perfectly camouflaged against the stone that it was invisible to the naked eye.

Bert was gobsmacked. 'How did you do that?' he asked.

'*The future is in your hands*,' said Ruby, twisting the handle. 'The priest told us!'

With a terrific groan of age-old hinges, a small door opened in front of them. Bert peered through into the gloomy candlelit corridor that lay ahead.

'Ruby, you're a genius!' he said. 'Come on.'

He took hold of her hand and pulled her down the passageway.

'Wait. Wait,' said Ruby, struggling free. 'What about Father Hooper? We can't just leave him here.'

'Hmm,' mumbled Bert. 'The priest.'

They turned back to the door, and froze. Father Hooper, still chanting, was walking towards the flames, his arms outstretched.

'Oh my God. No!' yelled Ruby, running out into the vault. 'Father Hooper!'

Suddenly Bert grabbed her and tugged her back. With a thundering roar, the vault ceiling collapsed, engulfing the priest in an avalanche of rubble. Clouds of smoke billowed through into the passageway, pushing Ruby and Bert back away from the vault door. Eventually, as the rocks stopped falling, the dust began to settle.

'Do you think he's still alive?' said Ruby, her mouth and throat dry with choking soot and dirt.

'I hope not,' said Bert, looking at the heap of stones and earth in front of them. Another low rumble shook the walls of the tunnel. 'I think it's time we left though.'

Ruby nodded. They turned and fled along the short passage to the vestry door, dodging the debris as it fell around them. Glancing at Ruby, Bert grasped the handle and twisted it. With a creak it opened.

'Phew,' said Bert.

'Let's get out here,' said Ruby.

They ran out through the vestry, up the spiral staircase and out into the small chapel, where the air was already thick with smoke. Their trainers squeaking on the tiled floor, they ran for the door and burst out into the daylight, gasping for fresh air. Coughing and choking, and white with dust and soot, they collapsed on to the grass.

Bert looked at his watch. 'It's just past eleven,' he wheezed. 'We've got four hours until the sun disappears.' He hauled himself to his feet and pulled Ruby up. 'And we haven't got time to rest. We've got to stop Whicker finding that pug dog.'

Ruby brushed the grass off her trousers.

'That's if he hasn't found it already.'

With the waves crashing against the rocks beneath them, and the seagulls wheeling overhead, Bert and

163

Ruby raced along the cliff path. Way ahead of them, out over the tussock grass, the Baloddan Hotel stood out against the skyline. Brightly coloured coaches bounced along the driveway, delivering tourists to the hotel, before they turned and headed back to the train station for another load.

Finally Bert and Ruby reached the gravel of the car park and stumbled, exhausted, towards the main doors. But as Bert was about to push his way through into the giant hallway, he stopped and stared through the glass. The foyer was heaving with a mass of people dressed in dinner jackets, ball dresses and glittering fake diamonds. An enormous banner hung over the grand staircase: 'WELCOME TO THE SOLAR ECLIPSE AT THE BALODDAN HOTEL'.

Ruby was panting behind him. 'Well, what are we waiting for?' she asked.

'Something the gaffer said,' said Bert, lost in his thoughts. 'He didn't want us to set foot back in the hotel.'

'When did he say that?' asked Ruby.

'Last night,' said Bert.

Ruby thought for a moment and then leant across, pushed one of the doors open and turned to glare at Bert. 'Well, we're not going to get far by hanging around out here, are we?' she said, pushing him over the threshold.

* * *

Inside the hall, the hubbub was deafening.

'How the hell are we going to find a pug dog in this lot?' asked Ruby over the noise.

More guests poured in through the doors behind them, forcing Bert and Ruby aside as they flooded towards the champagne and food.

'We find Captain Fabulous,' said Bert, stumbling forward.

'Who?' asked Ruby.

'Mr Dawbany, Elvis's owner. He'll be wearing a tight-fitting leotard with a cape. He should be easy to spot.'

Much to the disgust of many of the guests, Bert and Ruby squeezed themselves through the forest of bodies, carefully studying the clothing around them. Everyone was there, all the hotel staff, hundreds of guests, Bert's mum and dad, the Spanish cooks whose relatives had flown in for the occasion, everyone. Everyone, that is, other than Captain Fabulous.

'This is totally hopeless,' said Ruby finally.

'He must be here *somewhere*,' said Bert.

'No sign of Whicker either,' said Ruby.

'He'd have to be careful. His skin would have put people right off their food.'

Ruby looked about. 'And no sign of your grandfather.'

Bert spun round. 'The radio!' he gasped, hauling it out of his pocket. As he twiddled the button by the aerial, the radio popped and whistled. 'Grandpa? Grandpa, can you hear me?'

With a loud crackle, the gaffer's voice hissed to life. 'Robert? . . . uby? Thank goodness . . . need your . . .'

Bert waited as the radio hissed. 'Gaffer?' he said.

The machine popped and spat, and then a single word crackled out of the speaker.

'. . . basement.'

The radio died. Bert whacked it on the floor.

'Grandpa? Grandpa? Useless piece of home-made . . .'

Suddenly he got a nudge from Ruby. 'Look, Robert! Cats.'

Bert looked up to see a tail in front of him winding its way through the crowd. As he looked around him he spotted more tails. There were cats everywhere. Ginger cats, black and white cats, albinos, just like in the vault, all heading in the same direction towards the apartment door. Bert grabbed Ruby's hand and yanked it.

'Excuse me!' he shouted as he barged through the guests, knocking champagne glasses and vol-au-vents all over the sparkling outfits. 'Emergency!'

They broke out of the forest of legs and pushed through into the apartment. *Thwatthwat* went the door as it bounced back on its sprung hinges. Around them the stream of cats scurried into the quiet hallway and disappeared down the steps towards the first basement.

166

Ruby ran over and looked down into the darkness. 'Do you think the gaffer's definitely down there?' she asked.

Bert shook the radio. Nothing.

'Soon find out I suppose,' he said.

Shivering, they descended the staircase into the depths of the cold and gloomy first basement. The lights in the ceiling buzzed and flickered as condensation dripped from the lead pipes and collected in puddles on the flagstones around their feet.

'Shhh,' whispered Bert, as they wound their way through the dimly lit corridors, scampering after the line of cats.

'I can smell Whicker,' whispered Ruby, sniffing the air.

'Keep your eyes peeled,' said Bert, examining each corridor they passed. 'He's definitely around here somewhere.'

Finally, as they rounded a corner, they came to a wooden door, where the cats disappeared through a large crack by the floor.

'The boiler room,' whispered Bert. 'This is where the policeman got taken.' He pressed his ear against the door and listened. A high-pitched wailing could be heard over the low rumble of the boiler.

Turning around he took Ruby's hand. 'Ruby, whatever we find in here, however unpleasant, if there's any trouble you run for help,' he whispered. 'OK?'

'I'm not leaving here without you,' said Ruby.

'Just promise to do it.'

Ruby finally nodded. 'But where's your grandfather?' she asked.

Bert slowly turned the door handle. 'I don't know. But I hope he finds us quickly.'

The door swung open in front of them, revealing the swelteringly hot boiler room, lit by a single naked bulb that hung limply from the ceiling. The floor was a carpet of hissing, spitting cats.

Ruby started to back away. 'Jeez,' she said. 'I don't like the look of this.'

On the other side of the room, the pug dog had retreated under the tank and was growling at the advancing wall of livid, howling cats.

'Found the pug,' said Bert.

'Thank God,' muttered Ruby.

'Watch out for Whicker while I try to get to it.'

Ruby nervously kept an eye on the passage outside the door. 'I don't like this, Robert. Let's get out of here quickly.'

'Two more minutes.'

With the caterwaul of the animals around him, Bert fought his way to the boiler, leant underneath and heaved the squealing dog up into his arms.

'Careful it doesn't bite you,' said Ruby, grimacing as the dog excitedly licked Bert's face.

'Well,' said Bert, feeling almost as relieved as the dog looked, 'that was surprisingly easy.'

'Yes,' came a chilling voice from behind him. 'It was. Wasn't it?'

Bert spun round as Mr Whicker leapt down from the ceiling in the far corner of the room. As he landed in the light amongst the plague of cats, Bert could see the skin on his face had now started to peel away. His pockmarked hands were bubbling and steaming, and his lizard-like tongue darted out, tasting the air around him. Bert pressed himself up against the scalding hot boiler, as the dog fought to free itself from his arms.

Whicker shuffled up to him on all fours. 'Robert Twistleton, you're becoming a bit of a nuisance,' he whispered, his eyes sparkling in the light. Bert watched, terrified, as Whicker slimed closer, his foul, wafting stench almost making Bert retch. Suddenly the grocer lunged at him, stood up and flashed his green mouldy teeth. 'Of course, I have to thank you for pulling sweet little Elvis here out from his hiding place . . .' With a vicious snap, the dog went for his fingers. Whicker swept his hand away, '. . . a feat I was having some difficulty with.'

The door behind them slammed and Ruby's squeaking footsteps could be heard as she ran away down the passage.

'Run!' shouted Bert.

Whicker stood there laughing.

'Run, little girl, run!' he squealed. 'Oh, how touching. Your young girlfriend's gone for help.

169

Pointless of course, as by the time she gets back, you'll be *dead*.'

With a swipe of his hand, Whicker struck Bert across the face, sending him flying across the room through the sea of cats. With a thud, he hit the wall and let go of Elvis, who squeezed himself under a pipe.

'Did you honestly think you could stop me?' growled Whicker, stepping towards him and picking him up again by his sweater. 'You, a small child?'

With another strike, Bert was sent sliding across the floor, cutting a swathe through the carpet of hissing fur. His scratched face was starting to swell and bruise.

'What the hell are you?' Bert lisped as Whicker lurched towards him again and pulled him up against the wall.

'I'm your friendly local grocer,' Whicker whispered.

'You won't get away with this,' said Bert, the salty taste of blood swimming in his mouth. 'If *we* don't stop you, then my grandfather definitely will.'

With that Whicker bent back and roared with laughter. 'Your grandfather? Your pathetic grandfather?' He hoisted Bert up into the air and pinned him against the ceiling. 'You don't have a clue, do you?' he breathed, his menacing voice as deep as the rumbling boiler. 'You haven't a single idea what your grandfather's done? Well let me fill you in,' he said, his slimy purple tongue flicking across his teeth, 'on the *juicy* details.'

'Put him down, Whicker,' came a harsh voice from behind.

Whicker spun round. The gaffer was standing tall, silhouetted in the doorway like a superhero in a comic. He had a canvas bag in his arms, a strange-looking pack strapped to his back, and he wore a pair of thick gardening gloves.

'Well, well, well,' said Whicker, surprised, 'if it isn't the old fool himself.'

'Put my grandson down.'

Whicker let go of Bert, who fell into the mêlée of cats like a stone weight. With his eyes glowing red and his tongue darting in and out, Whicker stepped towards the door.

'So what do you plan to do, old man?' he rasped.

Bert watched as the gaffer pulled an extraordinary-looking machine from the duffle bag. Part vacuum, part gun, the contraption was attached to the backpack via a long silver tube.

Mr Whicker started to laugh. 'Ooh my, what's this?' he said, staring at the machine. 'Another pathetic invention? Let's hope it's a bit more effective than the insect repellent I sold you, eh?'

'Oh, it is,' said the gaffer, switching it on. With a reverberating hum, the machine on his back shook and started to glow a vibrant electric blue.

'Goodness!' sang Whicker. 'Pretty colours!'

Suddenly, as the gaffer pushed another button on the machine, the contraption leapt in his arms and expanded. The pack doubled in size as shocks of electric current surged down the silver hand piece. Whicker stopped smiling and stepped back towards the boiler.

'Why don't I give you a taster?' asked the gaffer. With a squeeze of the trigger, the machine shuddered, blasting a huge bolt of lightning from the nozzle and immediately frying a dozen cats at Whicker's feet. With the gagging stench of burnt fur, the machine then sucked them up through the hand piece and spat the cats' remains into the backpack. Bert was gobsmacked. Whicker looked terrified.

'Call it a home-made dust-buster,' said the gaffer, plainly a little surprised at the machine's effectiveness. 'I've been perfecting it for the best part of twenty years.'

'All those vacuum machines in that room under the fountain,' mumbled Bert.

'And those strange shopping lists you brought to the shop,' said Whicker. 'I knew you were up to something.' Whicker leapt up and clung on to the ceiling like a fly. 'But you won't stop me, Twistleton,' he screamed. 'It's too late now.'

Again the gaffer unleashed the machine, sending an arc of lightning across the room, missing Whicker by inches and punching a large, smoking hole in the ceiling. Whicker squealed as he leapt into the corner of the room, a mass of hissing cats following him, licking him and rubbing against him.

'Robert,' shouted the gaffer, 'get the dog.' Bert got to his feet and limped across the room. 'Quickly. We haven't got time to waste.' Bert scooped the whimpering dog out from underneath the pipe and hurried over to the door. Whicker hissed at him as he passed. 'One false move, Whicker. I'm warning you,' said the gaffer.

'Now what?' asked Bert, holding Elvis in his arms.

'Now leave us,' said the gaffer, not taking his eyes off the corner of the room.

'But I can't leave you here with this . . . thing.'

'This *thing*'s got a lot to answer for.'

Whicker chuckled in the corner. 'So *I'm* the only guilty one, am I?' he croaked. 'How about telling your grandson the part *you* played in all this? How you built the hotel in full knowledge of what it was going to hide.'

Bert frowned at his grandfather.

'Go, Robert!' shouted the gaffer. 'Find the beast. I'll catch you up after I've dealt with *this* reptile.'

Whicker flashed his eyes at Bert. 'Why don't you ask your grandfather who the beast really is, Robert?' he said. 'Ask him what he's got to hide!'

'Grandpa?'

'Go!' shouted the gaffer. Bert opened the door and hurried out into the passage.

'Ask him about true love, Robert,' screamed Whicker, cackling with laughter. 'Ask him now, as you'll never see him again!'

Suddenly a terrific zapping sound shook Bert. The walls around him flashed with blue as the gaffer unleashed the full power of the machine on Whicker. With the pug dog in his arms, Bert ran down through the passageways, Whicker's howling ringing in his ears.

Suddenly Ruby stepped out in front of him, almost causing him to fall over. 'Robert, are you OK?'

'Yes, yes. I think so,' hurried Bert, his face bruised and his clothes torn. 'The gaffer saved me.'

'I know,' said Ruby. 'I came across him down here with that weird machine when I ran for help. It seemed like he was hesitating. Waiting for something to happen.'

Bert looked confused. 'There's something the gaffer hasn't told us, Ruby,' he said. 'Something Whicker said . . .'

ZAP. The walls around them flashed blue again as the bolts of electric current could be heard snapping behind them.

'Do you think your grandfather needs a hand?' panicked Ruby.

'No. He said we should get on and find the lair. We're running out of time.'

'What *is* the time?'

Bert pressed the buttons on his watch. 'We've got forty minutes,' he said.

'OK. So. We have the dog,' said Ruby. Elvis was trembling in Bert's arms. 'Now what?'

Bert examined Elvis, turning the pug dog around in his hands as if it was some sort of domestic appliance.

'I can't work out this key thing,' he said, studying Elvis's flabby, hairless underbelly. 'There's nothing on him, not even a collar.'

'Maybe the key's, er . . .' Ruby smiled awkwardly as she pressed her hands over the dog's ears, '. . . inside him.' Elvis looked worried. Ruby stroked his head comfortingly.

'You think we're supposed to look inside?' said Bert, horrified. Elvis's concern now turned to panic. 'I'm not very good at biology,' said Bert, studying Elvis's bottom. 'Which end would we go through?'

Ruby grimaced. 'On second thoughts, maybe Elvis is the key himself,' she said. 'That's what the writing in the vault suggested. I think we should try that, before we go . . . well, you know.'

'OK, you're right,' said Bert. 'So we squash him through a keyhole?'

Behind them more zapping could be heard. Ruby kept glancing over to the boiler room door.

'Look, I've got one main concern,' she said nervously. 'Let's say we *do* find this door or exit thing, and successfully unlock it . . .'

'Right.'

'Well, if we open it, we let the beast out. And then everyone gets eaten.'

Bert thought for a moment. 'Whicker said that the beast only fully matures at the eclipse,' he said. 'If we get down to it, wherever it is, *before* the sun totally disappears, we can stop it before it bursts free.'

'You sound pretty sure of that,' said Ruby.

'Got any better ideas?' asked Bert.

The lights flickered and buzzed overhead as Ruby pondered for a moment. 'So where's the exit we have to unlock?'

'Right. The priest said the exit had to be huge,' said Bert. 'Big enough for the beast to get out of. And it must come up into the hotel somewhere.'

'So it's down here, in the basements,' said Ruby, looking about her. *ZAP*. 'Are you sure your grandfather doesn't need a hand?'

'No. Yes. He said he'd be OK. Look, the beast needs to get directly out where the food is. Right into the core of the hotel. So, we need to find the biggest space *in* the building.'

'That must be the main hall,' said Ruby. 'Where the guests are mingling before the eclipse.'

'Bingo!' said Bert.

Ruby turned in the direction of the stairs up to the apartment.

'No, this way,' said Bert, pointing up another dark,

rickety staircase. 'It'll be quicker.'

Together they darted up the stairs into the blackness, Ruby following Bert as he sped round the winding banisters. Eventually a tiny chink of light appeared ahead of them, and after a few more steps Bert stopped.

'Where are we?' asked Ruby, panting.

'Remember I told you these tunnels were originally used by the maids,' said Bert, 'so that they could get about the hotel without being noticed?'

'Yes.'

Bert pushed open a door in front of him. Ruby poked her head out into the light.

'We're in one of the hotel corridors,' said Ruby. They stepped out on to the carpet. 'And we've come straight out of a linen cupboard.'

'We're on the first floor,' said Bert. 'Good, isn't it?'

Ruby grabbed Bert's arm, and looked at his watch. 'Thirty-three minutes and counting.'

'Come on,' said Bert, and they started to jog down the passage. In front of them they could hear the hubbub of a large crowd of people.

'That must be the guests,' said Ruby.

'Yes.' Bert stopped. 'And I think they're coming this way. Hide!'

Bert opened a door and pushed Ruby through, leaving a chink to see back out into the corridor. They watched as Bert's mother, dressed in a long, flowing gown, glided past, followed by the entire crowd of excited guests in all their finery.

'Everyone up to the rooftop for champagne and hors d'oeuvres,' shouted Bert's mum haughtily. 'Only half an hour until total darkness.'

Eventually, as the last of the hundreds of guests surged past them chattering like school children, the corridor was left empty.

Bert stuck his head out to check they were alone. 'Come on,' he said, darting back out into the passage.

With the pug still in Bert's arms, they ran through the corridors until eventually they arrived at the top of the grand staircase. Together they looked out over the tiled hallway, now empty of hotel guests.

'OK, we need to find an enormous doorway,' said Bert, and he sprinted down the stairs. Hurriedly, he ran round the hall studying the walls as Ruby remained on the staircase. 'Are you just going to stand up there watching, or are you going to help?' shouted Bert as he circled the room.

'I'll be with you in a moment,' said Ruby, deep in thought.

Bert continued to search the hallway until finally he came to a halt in the centre of the tiled floor. 'Well?' he shouted up to Ruby.

'Robert,' said Ruby slowly, 'did your grandfather say the hotel was built directly over the remains of the monastery?'

'I think so,' said Bert. 'So what? What are you thinking?'

'And the priest said that he and the monks put a lock on the exit, right under Whicker's nose?'

'Right.' Bert frowned. 'Is this leading anywhere, or are you just waffling?'

'No, no,' said Ruby. 'I might have an idea.'

Bert looked at the walls around him. 'Don't tell me there's more of that Latin rubbish to work out?'

Ruby started laughing. 'No, but that's exactly what you'd expect. I think this is far simpler and quite brilliant. And what's more you're standing directly on top of it.'

Bert looked down at his feet. The floor beneath him was a mass of multicoloured floor tiles.

'You'll need to come up here,' shouted Ruby.

Bert raced back up the staircase and looked out over the hallway. 'I don't get it,' he said.

'Use your eyes,' said Ruby.

The floor of the hall was a vast mosaic, showing a scene of Baloddan harbour. All the boats and old buildings in the village were illustrated in great detail.

'I still don't get it,' said Bert.

Ruby took the dog out of Bert's arms and marched down the stairs, out over the tiled floor and stopped above a building where stacks of vegetables stood outside on the pavement. There in the window of what was plainly a shop stood the grocer himself.

'Right under Whicker's nose,' shouted Ruby, and she stamped on the tiles beneath her. They all sounded hard and ceramic, until she trod on the stone directly below Whicker's face. It sounded louder, as if it was made of wood. She bent down, lifted up the tile and found a hole, exactly the same size as Elvis.

'Oh my God,' shouted Bert as he raced down to join her. Ruby placed Elvis, petrified, in the hole. He didn't even struggle. 'This is incredible,' said Bert. 'Now what?'

Ruby shrugged.

Seconds flicked by without anything happening.

'I'm sure it must be right,' said Ruby. 'I mean he does seem to fit.'

Suddenly the ground started to shake beneath them.

'Hold on,' shouted Bert, as with a terrific groan the tiled floor started to turn and open, carrying them to the side of the room. Slowly, as the entire floor spun away, a vast hole opened up in front of them, leaving Bert and Ruby on the edge, looking straight down into a massive chasm.

'Oh my goodness,' said Bert, pressing himself against the wall. 'I think we found the door all right.'

Ruby didn't dare look down. 'I don't like heights, Robert,' she quivered.

Below them a vast pit had opened up, a giant hole that dropped down hundreds of feet. The stone walls of the chasm were intricately carved and lit by thousands of candles. Steps made from giant slabs of stone protruded from the walls and dropped down into the abyss. And far, far below, right at the base, another tiled floor could be seen, where a dot of a figure stood in the centre.

'Oh. My. Goodness,' said Ruby, desperate not to fall. 'What have we found?'

'Shhhhhhhh!' said Bert. 'I can hear something.'

There was a beautiful, eerie sound rising up from the depths, like a human voice, soft and lilting.

'Sounds like someone singing,' said Ruby. 'A hymn or something.'

'No,' said Bert, the toes of his shoes hanging out over the drop. 'That's a lullaby.'

Ruby turned and stared at Bert. 'You sound as if you know it?'

'I should,' he said. 'It's my grandmother singing.'

Chapter Twelve

'What's your grandmother doing hundreds of feet below the hotel singing lullabies when she's supposed to be dead?' Ruby asked Bert, the tips of her shoes hanging out over the precipice.

Tentatively, Bert leant out over the edge. 'Search me,' he said, immediately rocking back and clinging to the wall.

'She *is* dead, isn't she?' asked Ruby, manically staring straight ahead. 'I mean we went to her memorial. And you said you heard her go.'

'I did hear her go,' said Bert. 'She was sucked down the loo. Bottom first, according to the policeman.'

'Well, maybe that's not actually her singing then,' said Ruby. 'Maybe that's one of those replicas, like the librarian in the village.'

'Felicity Redmond?' said Bert. 'But we'd have seen Granny's double if she'd been taken and replaced. Just like we saw the Heaver sister after she was eaten down in that tunnel.'

'So it was just a freak loo-sucking incident, then, your granny's death?' asked Ruby.

'Must have been.'

'And she's definitely dead.'

'Think so.'

'Then what's she doing singing lullabies down there, then?'

Bert shivered. 'I don't know,' he said.

Around them the empty and now floorless hotel hallway seemed far bigger than it ever had before. And as Ruby momentarily looked out of the large windows towards the cliff path, her heart missed a beat. An eerie darkness, like an overcast day without a cloud in the sky, began to fall across the tussock grass. She nudged Bert.

'Whoa! Watch what you're doing!' he screamed, wobbling precariously.

'Look, the eclipse is starting,' said Ruby.

Bert peered out of the window. 'Oh God,' he said. He glanced at his watch. 'Fourteen minutes until total darkness. What do we do now?'

'We've got to get down there,' said Ruby.

183

'But I can't see any monster,' said Bert. 'Maybe the whole thing's a big mistake.'

The singing below them started to get louder.

'Where do you think the gaffer's got to?' asked Ruby, anxiously peering round the hallway.

'Not sure, but I wish he'd hurry up.'

Outside it was steadily getting darker.

'Robert, I think you should make a start,' said Ruby decisively. 'I'll wait up here for your grandfather. He's bound to turn up soon.'

Bert peered out over the edge again. 'Right. And what do I do when I get down there? Fight this thing with my bare hands?'

'If your grandfather turns up . . . I'm sure he'll do something.'

'Great,' said Bert. 'And if he doesn't turn up?'

'Hide and hope for the best.'

'Perfect,' said Bert, distinctly unimpressed. He peered over the edge again. 'OK, there's a step directly below us.'

'How are you going to get to it?'

'Jump, I think,' said Bert, trying to sound brave.

'OK,' said Ruby.

They both stared out ahead, desperately willing the gaffer to appear. Suddenly Ruby leant over and gave Bert a peck on the cheek. He turned scarlet. 'That's for luck,' she said.

'Thanks,' replied Bert and he closed his eyes and stepped off the ledge. He felt his stomach drop as he sailed through the air and landed with a thud on the giant slab of stone jutting out of the wall a few feet below.

'Robert?' came Ruby's voice above him. 'Are you all right?'

Bert opened his eyes. 'I'm alive,' he called back, his words echoing around him. He crawled to the edge of the step and peered over. 'Crikey,' he whispered, completely awestruck. The cavern below him was vast, the same width as the hallway but dropping hundreds of feet like a massive well. From above, what had originally looked like arches carved into the wall were actually thousands and thousands of doorways, making Bert feel like he was inside a giant honeycomb. Each doorway was lit with glowing white candles. 'You really should see this, Ruby,' he called out. 'It's beautiful.'

'I'd rather stay up here, thanks,' came the terse reply.

Bert got to his feet. He looked out along the curved wall, at the huge steps spiralling into the depths below. A wide gap lay between Bert and the next slab. 'I'm going to try and jump to the next step,' he shouted.

'Right,' called out Ruby. 'Just don't fall, as I'm not coming to get you.'

'Thanks,' muttered Bert. Holding his breath he took a short run-up and leapt across the gap. For a fleeting moment he was flying through the air, nothing holding him up and a hard, stone floor hundreds of feet below. With a thud, he landed on the next slab, his feet skidding on the rock, sending small fragments sailing over the edge and clattering down the wall beneath him.

'How are you doing?' called Ruby.

'Fine,' said Bert, wiping the sweat off his forehead. 'Just.'

Again and again he leapt from step to step, dropping deeper into the cavern. The natural light became more and more faint, and the candles stood out in the darkness around him like millions of winking stars. And as he dropped, the sweet singing grew louder as if his grandmother was calling him down into the gloom.

'OK, I reckon I'm halfway,' he shouted up, as he stood on a ledge, catching his breath. He waited for a reply. 'Ruby?' he shouted. Nothing. For the first time Bert felt completely alone.

The air temperature was dropping as he continued to descend the vast spiral staircase. Below him the bent over figure of his grandmother was becoming clearer in the dim candlelight. She was sitting huddled on a stool in the middle of the floor, gently rocking as she sang the lullabies that had so often sent him to sleep as a child. The floor was getting closer and closer, until finally, out of breath, he reached the last step and jumped down to the ground.

His heart thumping, he surveyed the huge cavern floor that now stretched out in front of him. Around the edges of the huge space, hundreds of doors led off in every direction, and way above him Bert could see the hole through the hallway floor and the faint daylight that shone through it. He peered about nervously for any sign of the beast, and then warily made the first tentative steps out towards his grandmother.

'Granny?' he whispered as he tiptoed across the tiles. His grandmother was facing away from him, stooped over as she rocked to and fro singing quietly. 'Granny, it's Robert,' Bert whispered. Still no answer. Constantly scanning the room around him, he crept closer, until finally he was only a few feet away from the stool. 'Granny, is that you?' he said.

Suddenly his grandmother stopped singing and sat up. 'Robert?' she said, her voice warm and comforting. Bert's heart leapt and he ran the last few steps, flinging his arms out wide, ready to hug her. And just as he was about to wrap himself around her shoulders, he caught a flash of her hand as it rested on her knee. He stopped dead. The skin was pockmarked like Mr Whicker's, bubbling, oozing and steaming.

'Granny?' he said, his voice faltering slightly. And then she turned around to face him.

Bert recoiled in shock. Her once beautiful face was now purple and spotted like a chameleon's, with layers of slimy skin peeling away from her nose. And as her twitching eyes flashed red, she flicked her long green tongue across her teeth, and leant forward to give her grandson a kiss. Bert pulled back in revulsion, as his granny hissed with laughter.

'Well?' came a familiar, cold voice from behind him. 'Aren't you going to give your grandmother a kiss?'

The hairs on Bert's neck stood on end as he slowly turned round to see Mr Whicker standing right behind him. His skin and clothes were as black as charcoal and his hair was smoking, singed to a crisp. And in his steaming, burnt hand he held the gaffer's lightning machine.

'Where's my grandfather?' asked Bert, nervously backing away. 'What have you done to him?'

'Oh, I'm sorry,' said Mr Whicker, hobbling towards him. 'Your grandfather was unable to join us.' He dropped the machine to the floor and kicked it sliding across to Bert. 'But he sends his regards all the same.' He started to circle Bert, a trail of smoke wafting behind him as he hobbled from foot to foot. 'Mind you,' he said, glancing at Bert through the corner of his eye, 'I'm sure he'd be delighted to see that you've met up with your grandmother again.'

Bert looked at the bubbling mass crouched on the stool in the centre of the room. Fat, with liquid oozing and squirming under her waxy, translucent skin, she sang quietly to herself as she rocked back and forth.

'That isn't my grandmother,' said Bert.

'Oh, I'm afraid it is, Robert,' said Whicker. 'This beautiful old lady is the very same debutante your grandfather fell in love with all those years ago.' He coughed and sent a ball of green spittle smacking on to the floor. 'Of course we hid her real identity from him to begin with,' he choked, 'didn't want Godfrey running away too quickly. And then when he started to suspect the truth, how Edith here was eating her way through the hotel staff, he didn't have anywhere to turn. He'd built her the vast hotel she was using as a larder. The guilt kept him from spilling the beans.' He started to chuckle. 'That and a few veiled threats against his family. Isn't love a wonderful thing, Robert?'

'You're lying,' said Bert. 'You're lying. This isn't my grandmother. She can't have eaten all those people.'

'Oh, she has quite a voracious appetite,' said Whicker as he hopped to the centre of the room. He stroked Bert's granny lovingly, like a pet, as he stared adoringly into her eyes. 'And isn't it fabulous that so many of her victims could be with us here today?'

Suddenly Bert sensed thousands of eyes burning into his back. He looked up and gasped as he found that every one of the doorways in the wall above him had a figure standing in it, staring down at them silently. There were thousands of people, all with their faces lit by the millions of candles around them. Bert recognized some of the faces he could make out: Mr Tuttle, Miss Crankshaft the keep fit instructor, all three Heaver sisters, Felicity Redmond, even the police officer. It reminded him of the photographs that he'd found in his grandfather's hidden room. They were all standing dead still, silent, as if the life had been sucked out of them.

'And they've all come to witness this moment, to worship your grandmother in her true glory, and then to be devoured as a snack before she reaches the hotel guests on the surface.' Whicker chuckled as he rubbed his hands together in glee.

'You can't let this happen,' pleaded Bert. 'There's hundreds of innocent people up there. My family's up there.'

'Not all your family,' wheezed the grocer. 'Say hello to your father, Robert.'

Bert spun round to find his father standing, lifeless, in a doorway a few feet above him. 'Dad?' he said, taking a step towards him.

Whicker hopped into his path. 'Your grandmother just got a little peckish,' he said flippantly. 'Couldn't help herself.'

With anger rising inside him, Bert lunged at Whicker. But the grocer was too quick.

'Now, now, Robert,' he said playfully. 'There's no

time for fun and games. Maybe later.'

Suddenly the daylight from way up in the hotel disappeared completely, leaving only the candles giving out a dim, eerie light. Shadows danced across the floor as Bert looked at his watch in terror. Three ten exactly.

'Total darkness,' he whispered to himself.

'That's right,' said Whicker, crouching down to him. A terrible smile slowly crept across his face. 'Show time!'

Bert's grandmother immediately rocked forward and with a dreadful tearing, her clothes and skin started to split. Suddenly a terrific geyser of black slime erupted out of her shoulders, covering the surrounding walls in muck. And as gunge seeped out across the floor, a beast, dripping in mucus, unfolded from his grandmother's body like a butterfly freeing itself from its fat cocoon.

'Isn't she beautiful?' screamed Whicker as the horrific monster rapidly expanded, spewing pools of purple and green slime across the tiled floor. Bert stumbled backwards as, already towering above him, the beast continued to grow, its brown, pulsating skin slimy and pockmarked like a toad's. 'That's it, my precious, rise up and take what is yours!' Whicker wailed, waving his arms like an excited TV evangelist.

Now as tall as a tower block, and looming way above him, the creature resembled a vast mucus-covered sloth; its smooth, bald body raw like a newborn baby. Recoiling as it drew in a massive breath, the monster flexed its muscles and let out an ear-splitting roar, shaking the walls of the enormous cavern and sending huge boulders crashing down to the floor. Bert retreated under the arch of a doorway as, slowly, the vile beast spread out its four limbs and began to climb the walls towards the hotel, flicking its tongue out as it rose up, swallowing the people standing in the doorways.

As Bert watched, horrified, Whicker danced in the centre of the floor, screaming with laughter. Bert knew that his moment for saving the hotel was slipping away from him. Soon his family and friends would be devoured and the hotel above him destroyed. Quite suddenly though, as he stood there, watching in horror, he thought he heard his grandfather's voice inside his head.

'Do something, Robert,' it whispered.

Bert looked at the floor beside him. Lying down by his feet was his grandfather's electricity machine. He wondered if it still worked. Slowly, so as not to gain Whicker's attention, he picked it up and slipped the pack on to his back. As soon as he did so, two mechanical arms clamped either side of his waist, squeezing him as if the pack itself was holding on. Wondering how to turn it on, he examined the long chrome tube in his hands. On the handle he found the power button with 'Danger, gloves needed' flashing above it. Bert didn't have any gloves. With

Whicker whooping and dancing in front of him like a crazed game show host, and the creature climbing higher and higher, Bert closed his eyes and pressed the power button. The pack on his back jolted and glowed bright blue.

Now lit up like a Christmas tree, Whicker turned to him and frowned. For a second he remained speechless until slowly he started to laugh. 'You think you can stop your grandmother with that thing?' he spat. 'You couldn't swat a fly with that!'

'That's not my grandmother,' said Bert. He pushed another button and electric shocks surged down the hand piece, making his hands shudder and burn whilst the pack on his back shook violently and expanded. The beast was getting higher and higher, climbing ever closer to the hallway exit.

'Give it to me, child,' said Whicker, as he crept towards him with his hands out. 'You don't want to repeat what happened to your grandfather, do you?'

Bert reckoned he needed to hit the beast right between the eyes with a direct shot if he had any chance of stopping it. To do that he'd have to get the creature to face him, but how? He racked his brain.

Whicker, meanwhile, was starting to look more and more concerned. 'You know you haven't got the guts to even try it,' he rumbled, but he was plainly nervous about getting too close.

Think, Robert, think, Bert kept saying to himself. Get the beast to turn around.

'You're just like your pathetic grandfather,' hissed Whicker. 'He didn't have the guts to finish me off before I snapped the machine out of his hands and gave him a dose of his own medicine.' He took a step closer and smiled sweetly. 'Give the machine to me, there's a good boy.'

And then, quite suddenly, the answer came to Bert. Taking a deep breath, he started to sing. Like a songbird, he filled his lungs and sang the very lullaby that his grandmother had sung to him. And as the beautiful, lilting melody rose up towards the hotel hallway, the creature stopped dead in its tracks. It turned round to face Bert, its horrible features warty and disfigured, with saliva dripping from its mandibles. And that instant Bert's heart fell, as he recognized his loving grandmother behind the creature's glowing eyes.

'Forgive me,' he whispered, and with a squeeze of the trigger he unleashed a thunderous bolt of electricity straight for the beast's forehead.

The force of the recoil immediately hit Bert like a juggernaut, blasting him backwards, sending him sliding across the floor. With a terrific thud he slammed against the wall, as above him the creature screamed in pain.

Whicker looked up, horror written across his face. 'What have you done?' he yelled in disbelief, as above him the beast started to lose its hold. His eyes had turned a vibrant red against his black, burnt skin, as around him huge boulders started to rain down, crashing on to the tiled floor. 'What the hell have you done?'

With a bloodcurdling roar, the beast fell, its huge bulk careering towards the ground. 'You'll pay for this Twistleton!' screamed Whicker as he watched the scorched monster thundering towards him.

Suddenly the candles around Bert blew out, as the down-draught blasted open the doors at the base of the walls. And then, just like one of the candles, Bert blacked out.

A fortnight later

Bert opened one eye. Brilliant sunshine hit him like a sledgehammer. He closed it tight again. His head felt sore and he couldn't move. Where was he?

'Robert?'

He could hear seagulls, boat rigging chattering in the breeze, the murmur of people talking . . .

'Robert? Are you awake?'

Bert opened an eye again. Ruby's smiling face was inches in front of him.

'Oh my God. You're awake,' she said excitedly. 'Can you hear me?'

He tried to sit up.

'No, no, don't move. You'll pull the drips out of your arm.'

'My head hurts,' he whispered. His mouth felt dry, his tongue furry.

'Your head's going to hurt for quite a while,' she said.

'I'd like a drink of water.'

'OK, right. I'll get a nurse,' she said. Then she stopped. 'Oh, there's just one thing. Can you remember anything that happened?'

Bert thought back. He could picture his father standing in a doorway, and Whicker screaming at him, and the hole in the hallway floor.

'Sort of,' he said.

'Well, keep it to yourself, Robert. Don't talk about it.' She looked about, checking that no one could hear her. 'You'll find out why.'

'Well,' came a chirpy, unfamiliar voice suddenly, 'look who's finally woken up?'

Bert peered out from underneath the bandages around his head. A nurse had marched into the room and was now glaring at him from the foot of the bed.

'Mrs Twistleton, your son's awake,' she called as she walked round to him. He felt a pair of arms grip him around the waist, and slowly he was pulled up the mattress into a sitting position. 'That's better,' said the nurse.

Bert looked about. He was in a large, bright room that overlooked the harbour. Sunshine poured in through the window, and beside him sat Ruby. She winked at him.

'Robert?' came his mother's voice as she marched in through the doors. Tallulah floated in behind her. 'Robert? My boy.' His mum rushed up to him and gave him a kiss on the forehead. Bert recoiled in pain. Tallulah sat on the end of the bed, and stared at him, as if she was looking at a stranger. 'Thank goodness you're all right,' sighed his mother.

'How about Dad?' whispered Bert. 'Is he OK? I saw him.'

His mum went quiet and squeezed his hand. Tallulah's eyes filled with tears. She fiddled with a handkerchief and stared out of the window.

Suddenly the nurse leant over and pulled the bandages out of his eyes. 'Right, let's see if we can smarten you up a bit, now that you've finally decided to be with us. I think a wash is in order.'

'What happened to the hotel?' asked Bert.

His mum cleared her throat. 'The basements collapsed, Robert. Under the main hall. Your father and I always worried they would. You were caught in the fall. We'd have lost you too if you hadn't been dragged out.'

'And Grandpa?'

Tallulah got up and disappeared out through the door as his mum shook her head slowly. 'We found a letter he'd left for you in his desk,' she said weakly. She wiped a tear away and rested the envelope on the bed sheet. 'He always did feel close to you, Robert.'

Bert's eyes started to well up.

'Mrs Twistleton, we're going to give Robert a bit of a spring clean,' said the nurse quietly. 'Make him comfortable. Maybe you could come back in half an hour, the doctor will be coming to visit Robert then.'

Bert's mum nodded. As she got up, she leant over and kissed her son again. 'We've got you though. We're not going to let go of you.' She smiled. 'We'll be outside,' she said. 'Not far away.' And she disappeared through the door.

Ruby pulled herself out of the chair. 'I'll be back later too,' she said. 'These nurses have looked after you for nearly two weeks, Robert, so don't be too grouchy with them.' She leant over to give him a peck on the cheek. 'Keep quiet,' she whispered, 'about . . . you know.'

The nurse saw Ruby out of the room, and Bert picked up and opened the envelope lying beside him. Sliding his finger under the flap, he took out the sheet inside, inquisitive as to what his grandfather might have written in a letter.

'Dear Robert,' the note read. Bert reorganized the tubes coming out of his arm. 'By the time you receive this I shall be dead. There were many things I should have told you, so many things we should have discussed man to man.' He pushed the bandage up out of his eyes. This letter was getting weird already. 'As you read this note, many of the questions you had will now have been answered. My failures in life will have become apparent. Don't be angry at your grandmother, Robert. I loved her once. However, there is one thing that you should have been told; one thing that I am guilty of not facing up to.' OK, now the letter was getting really weird, he thought. 'You were your grandmother's favourite, Robert, and for good reason. You are the next in line. You were chosen over your father. The creature is inside you, a part of you. You are the next Beast of Baloddan.'

Bert frowned, and looked about. He half expected his grandfather to jump round the door laughing. This must have been a joke after all.

'A long future lies in front of you, Robert, with plenty of difficult decisions. Good luck, my dear grandson, and may fate smile on you. With love, Gaffer.'

Bert couldn't believe it. He started to read it again.

Suddenly the nurse reappeared. 'OK, you're going to have some company in here today, Robert. Another patient. The room's a bit too big and sunny to have all to yourself. Then we'll get you cleaned up.'

Two porters appeared, pushing a bed into the ward. Bert couldn't see who was lying in it; the pillows hid any signs of a face.

'Mind you,' said the nurse, 'I expect you'll have a lot to talk about. This is the gentleman that saved you, Robert.' Bert frowned again. 'You owe this man your life.'

Then he clicked. The letter *was* a joke. 'Gaffer?' he said, trying to peer over the pillows as the bed was wheeled beside him. 'My grandfather saved my life, I knew it,' he said to the nurse.

But suddenly the patient rolled over. Bert's heart missed a beat as, instead of his grandfather, a charcoaled, burnt face peered out at him.

'Mr Whicker,' whispered Bert, falling back into his pillow. 'The protector . . . of the beast.'

'Just call me a doting nanny,' said Whicker, flashing Bert a smile.

THE MEMORY PRISONER

Thomas Bloor

Maddie stood for a while, staring out into the street. She felt, as she always did when confronted by a open door, as if she was standing on the edge of a precipice overlooking a bottomless ocean . . .

Maddie is fifteen and overweight. She hasn't left the house for thirteen years, since her grandfather disappeared.

Burying her memories, Maddie can't face her deepest fears. Until her brother's life is in danger – and she must leave her familiar prison behind, or lose him for good . . .

A Fidler Award-winning novel

'Subversive, funny and imaginative' *The Observer*

'Bizarrely comic' *The Guardian*

'Moving, alarming and funny' Jan Mark, *TES*